Reclaiming Our Forever

CIMARUTA MC CHICAGO
BOOK 2

NATALIE ARTHUR

The Cimaruta MC Chicago Series books are all stand alone with NO cheating and HEA.

Even though they are standalone, they are best enjoyed if read in order. There is also mention of characters from my Mancini Legacy Series.

❀ Created with Vellum

This is dedicated to everyone back on my island of Maui. #MauiStrong #LahainaStrong

Acknowledgments

Danni, this journey is so crazy! Thank you for being here with me!

Jessica, you are summer and I am winter. Always.

JD, thank you for spending late nights with and making sure I listened even when I didn't want to. Love you.

Kristen, we can do this. Together.

Nicole, I'm forever grateful that you're in my life.

Carissa, thank you for everything you do.

Mary, Tammy and Gretchen thank you for everything. For loving my books and supporting me.

Arthur, you've always supported me no matter how crazy my ideas are. I love you so much.

Mom, you've always been my biggest supporter and I don't know where I'd be without you.

Caoimhe-Lea, you drive me absolutely fucking crazy. But I wouldn't have it any other way. Love you.

Taye, and everyone I'm forgetting who has supported my crazy ideas and continue to be with me, thank you. I truly couldn't do this without all of you.

No part of this book or graphics were made with AI.
HUMAN CREATION ONLY

Reclaiming Our Forever has NO cheating with a guaranteed HEA. It is book two of my Cimaruta MC Chicago Series and is connected to my Mancini Legacy Series.

There are not a lot of dark moments or dark issues in my books, there still are the occasions that have to do with kidnapping, domestic abuse, and assault.

Check out my website for current news and trigger warnings.
Mancini Legacy and Cimaruta MC family trees.
Nataliearthurbooks.com

Mancini Legacy and Cimaruta MC Dictionary

Cage - Motorized vehicle with four wheels. (Cars)

Chicago Panthers - Professional baseball team.

Chicago Redhawks - Professional hockey team.

Cimaruta MC, Chicago - Chicago Motorcycle club, Mother charter

Cut - Vest that patched in members of the MC wear to identify who they are and their rank.

Lake Renegade Township - Town owned by the Mancini family.

Lucciola Island - 'Firefly' Island, owned by the Mancini family and located in Massachusetts.

Lucciola Memorial Hospital - Hospital in Lake Renegade Township.

Mancini Grill - 5-star restaurant located inside the Legacy Hotel.

Rockers - Top rocker has the club's name on it, the bottom rocker has the club's location.

Sprite Lake Village - Town in Illinois, owned by the Laurent family.

The Legacy Hotel - Hotel in downtown Chicago owned by the Mancini family.

Galway - Town in Ireland.

<u>ITALIAN</u>

Amore - Love.

Coglione - Asshole.

Colomba mia - My dove.

Cugino - Cousin.

Cuore mio - My heart.

Dolcezza - Sweetness.

Famiglia - Family.

Figlio - Son.

Fratello - Brother.

Il mio mondo - My world.

Il mio pinguino - My penguin.

Mai Andato - Never Gone.

Mi dispiace - I'm sorry.

Mi passerotta - My little sparrow.

Nonno - Grandfather.

Nonna - Grandmother.

Ti abbiamo aspettato - We waited for you.

Ti voglio bene - I love you.

Zio - Uncle.

Zia - Aunt.

IRISH

Aintín - Aunty

Is í Gàidhlig ár gcéad teanga - Gaelic is our first language.

M'anam - My soul

Mo stór - My treasure.

FRENCH

D'accord petite sœur - Okay little sister

Je t'aime et Lorenzo - I love you and Lorenzo

Je t'aime - I love you

Je vous aime tous les deux - I love you both

Princesse - Princess

Toujours - Always

Toujours mes frères - Always my brothers

Tu es ma princesse - You are my princess

FAUSTO & LUNA
GRANDPARENTS
GIACOMO
SON
CAITRÍONA
DAUGHTER IN LAW
CELESTINO
GRANDSON
FRANCESCO
GRANDSON
SAOIRSE
GREAT GRANDDAUGHTER
ISABELLA
GRANDDAUGHTER
LUCIANA
GRANDDAUGHTER
GRAYSON
GREAT GRANDSON
BASTIANINI
FAMILY

KEARNEY FAMILY

Liam & Orfhlaith
GRANDPARENTS

Caitríona
DAUGHTER

Giacomo
SON IN LAW

Celestino
GRANDSON

Francesco
GRANDSON

Saoirse
GREAT GRANDDAUGHTER

Isabella
GRANDDAUGHTER

Luciana
GRANDDAUGHTER

Grayson
GREAT GRANDSON

GIACOMO
CAITRÍONA
CELESTINO
ISABELLA
FRANCESCO
LUCIANA
MAEVE
RÓNÁN
SAOIRSE
GRAYSON
BASTIANINI
FAMILY

Ardghal +
Niamh
O'CALLAGHAN
Keegan
Aodhán
Fintan
Rónán
Luciana
Grayson

Cimaruta MC

President - Giacomo 'Forza' Bastianini

Vice President - Celestino 'Giustizia' Bastianini

Sgt-At-Arms - Francesco 'Bestia' Bastianini

Treasurer - Luciana 'Fuoco' Bastianini

Secretary - Isabella 'Dolce' Bastianini

Historian - Caitríona 'Forte' Bastianini

Road Captain - Connor 'Azrael' Byrne

Chaplain - Brennan 'Raziel' Doyle

Enforcer - Liam 'Amante' Murphy

Enforcer - Valentino 'Ombra' Marconi

Enforcer - Romana 'Fantasma' Vietti

Enforcer - Mitchell 'Granchio' Harris

Enforcer - Hollis 'Cavallo' Taylor

Enforcer - Rónán 'Ghiaccio' O'Callaghan

Enforcer - Fintan 'Toro' O'Callaghan

Prospect - Anthony Grimes

MANCINI FAMILY

Pietro & Alessia
Grandparents

Enea (T)
Son

Antonio (T)
Son

Leonardo (T)
Son

Gráinne
Daughter-in-law

Rosaura
Daughter-in-law

Sebastiano*
Grandson

Salvatore^
Grandson

Domenico*
Grandson

Fiorella^
Granddaughter

Lorenzo+
Grandson

Gianluca^
Grandson

Giovanna+
Granddaughter

Rowan
Great Grandson

(T) = Triplets

* = Twins

+ = Twins

^ = Triplets

MANCINI FAMILY

Contents

Chapter 1   1
Chapter 2   11
Chapter 3   23
Chapter 4   33
Chapter 5   43
Chapter 6   53
Chapter 7   63
Chapter 8   73
Chapter 9   85
Chapter 10   97
Chapter 11   107
Chapter 12   119
Chapter 13   131
Chapter 14   145
Chapter 15   155
Chapter 16   165
Chapter 17   173
Chapter 18   189
Chapter 19   195
Chapter 20   205
Chapter 21   219
Chapter 22   231
Chapter 23   239
Chapter 24   247
Chapter 25   257
Chapter 26   263
Chapter 27   269
Epilogue   277

About the Author   283

Also by Natalie Arthur   285

Reclaiming Our Forever

Chapter One

Francesco

Crazy. That's the only way to describe these last few months.

A few months ago, my baby sister Luciana was kidnapped by one of our chapter clubs from England. The now ex-president of the Feral Raptors, Richard 'T-Rex' Vaughan, and a few of his council members thought it was a good idea. She was gone for two fucking days. That may not seem like a long time, but to us? It felt like a lifetime. Not knowing if she was okay was the worst part.

After we found Luciana, we gave the remaining Raptors two choices: stand with us and kick out the members that backed their old president, or be voted out of the family. Their decision was to get rid of all the members that were loyal to T-Rex. When they were done cleaning house, they voted their road captain, Scrapper, in as president. He was the one that told us about T-Rex's plan to take my sister and kept us up on his movements. When it was all over, he asked to be given a chance to prove the Raptor's loyalty to the Cimaruta. Even though they have a new council and have gotten rid of the traitors, they're still on probation. My papà hasn't decided how long it will last, though. The biggest issue is knowing the remaining members will be supportive of Scrapper taking over. And making sure they're loyal to the Cimaruta.

Our club, the Cimaruta MC, Chicago, is the mother club, which means we're the original club. It was founded by my grandfathers, Fausto 'Drago' Bastianini and Liam 'Iolar' Kearney. They came from Italy and Ireland to make a better life for my parents.

When we turned eighteen, my fraternal twin brother, Celestino, and I prospected for the Cimaruta like everyone else in our club had to. Just because we're legacy doesn't mean we get special treatment. A few years later, we were voted onto the council. Besides prospecting, college wasn't something either of us wanted to do at the time. So we started our company, Magic Nights Chicago. We're male entertainers. Okay fine, we're strippers. But 'male entertainers' sounds more classy. We do shows Friday and Saturday nights at Luminescence—the club we co-own with the Mancini Mafia. We also do private shows.

Our Irish grandparents own our Magic Nights

company. It was the best option for us when we started our business because we were going through so many changes with our MC. Only a few of the dancers that work with us know that my grandparents own the company. We don't want any of the guys to feel like we're above them or that they need to 'answer' to us. We're all equals when it comes to working at the club.

Our MC has been going through major changes over the last seven years. We've gone from being on the wrong side of the law to being tax paying, law-abiding, motorcycle riders. At least ninety percent of the time, anyway.

When my twin and I were ten years old, our grandfathers stepped down as co-presidents of the Cimaruta MC, Chicago. They returned to their respective countries and started chapters there. Nonno Fausto started his in Florence, Italy and Granda Liam in Galway, Ireland—both of them keeping the Cimaruta name.

We visited Ireland and Italy once a year while we were growing up. But after my grandfathers moved back permanently, we went every few months.

In the last five years, only our parents have made the trip, so I'm excited to be back in Ireland and to see my Irish club brothers. My Granda Liam pops in whenever he feels like it even though he's not on their council anymore. But trust me when I say no one goes against anything he says. The same goes for our Florence, Italy chapter and Nonno Fausto. It doesn't matter that they're no longer the presidents of those chapters, they'll always be the founders of our MC. So that demands respect from all past, present and future club members.

The council members of our chapter clubs in other countries are required to join us in Chicago twice a year. Council members of our US chapters are required to attend every barbecue. Our club pays for half of all airfare, or if they choose to drive, half of their gas and lodging along the way. The rest comes out of their club coffers. Patched members are required to come to at least six functions a year if they live in the US, and at least one if they live abroad.

We usually have the barbecues that involve the chapters abroad in the spring and fall. It's a beautiful time of year in Chicago with the leaves turning, and the air is lighter. There are times when chapter clubs can't make it to the barbecues, even the mandatory ones. When that happens, we use the program that Sebastiano Mancini, of the Mancini Mafia, created called 'Script.' It's a video-chat program that also allows us to live stream everything that's going on and keep a recording of it.

Whenever we travel to either country, the first thing we do when we land is head over to see our grandparents. Then it's on to meet with the MC chapters.

My siblings and I have always been close. Celestino and I are a year older than Isabella and Luciana. When we were little, my mom told Celestino and me that we needed to watch over our little sisters. So we decided that we each had to watch one of them. Celestino chose Isabella and I chose Luciana. Wherever we went, they went.

It was always a lot of fun when we would go to the different clubhouses with our parents. The brothers in the club always made time to hang out with all four of us. We would swim in the ponds or play hide and seek in the trees. We spent so many summers learning about our Italian and Irish cultures.

When I was fourteen, I met the love of my life. She stole my heart the minute I saw her. And I knew from that moment on that there would never be anyone else for me.

This time when we land in Ireland, checking in with our MC chapter is put on hold for a couple of days. When we land today, we're going to be meeting Rónán's family. Then tomorrow, my baby sister Luciana is being proposed to—and she has no idea.

Our whole family is here for it, as well as the family of her soon-to-be fiancé, Rónán O'Callaghan. His parents own a restaurant located on the Aran Islands here in Ireland. My parents are thrilled because they love Rónán. Although that wasn't the case when he started dating Luciana...but he's proven how much he loves my sister and that he'd do anything for her. For us, that's all that matters.

Rónán has three older brothers, Keegan, Aodhán and Fintan. As of right now, all four of them are prospecting with us. Along with all of the Mancini kids. Well 'kids' isn't really the right word—we're all around the same age. There are seven of them. So our club is growing, and my papà is very happy. It's the first time in a long while that the club will gain this many members.

<u>Maeve</u>

I loved growing up in Ireland. I'm an only child, but my parents never made me feel like one. They were only children too, so they understood what it was like for me and always made sure I was happy. My da was the road captain for the Cimaruta MC, Galway Chapter. That means he took care of mapping out any runs that the club did, and he was in charge of everyone's was safety as well.

When I was fourteen years old, I found my soulmate. Francesco Liam Bastianini. We met at a club barbecue. He was six feet tall with beautiful blue-green eyes. They reminded me of the ocean. Whenever we would go out, girls would always flirt with him. But he never acted like he saw them. Only me.

The first time my life fell apart was when my parents died. I was sixteen, and they were out for a ride. A car crossed into their lane and hit them head on. I still remember that day like it was yesterday.

Because my da was a high-ranking officer on the Cimaruta council, the president of the Galway chapter came to tell me. That man was Francesco's grandfather. I was at home when he came to give me the news. I'll always be grateful Francesco was there with me that day. I don't know what I would've done if I had been alone when I found out. Besides Franco, my parents were all I had, and I lost them in the blink of an eye. There was no one to take care of me after they were gone. Well, I had my nana _ my da's mam, but she was sick. She made sure I had a place to live so that I didn't go into foster care, but beyond that, she couldn't do much. And that was okay, I loved her for doing that much for me. Liam made sure I knew that I would always have help from the club, no matter what I needed.

Two years later, my life fell apart again and this time it felt like I would never recover. Francesco left me, with no reason or explanation. After four years and all the promises we made to each other that we would always be together, he blindsided me. We texted every day, talked on the phone every day, even got to visit each other several times a year. The last visit, we got to spend our eighteenth birthdays together. After he left, the number of phone calls started to decrease. He would say that he got busy and he was so sorry. Then the texts became sporadic. The last time I spoke to him, he said everything was okay. That we were okay. He was just busy because he was prospecting for the Cimaruta, and starting a business with his twin brother, Celestino. But I had nothing to worry about because I was everything to him and we were going to spend the rest of our lives together.

Obviously, that was a lie. A few months later, I found out I was pregnant. I struggled with telling Francesco about it, but I didn't want him to come back just because of my pregnancy. There was never any other option but for me to have the baby.

A couple months after I found out I was pregnant, I met Callum McGregor. He had just moved here from Scotland and came into the cafe where I was working. He came in every night for dinner and always sat in my section. I was starting to show, but he never asked questions. We talked about life and things that he wanted to do now that he was in Ireland. I was about seven months pregnant when Callum asked me to have dinner with him. I told him I appreciated his offer but I couldn't accept. When he asked me why, I told him it wasn't something I could talk about. Then he asked me about the da of my baby. I told him that he wasn't in the picture. He told me that even if I wasn't ready to date him, I didn't have to do it all by myself.

That was the first time since Francesco left me that I didn't feel empty and alone. I'm not sure why, but when I met Callum, I felt like I could trust him. But that didn't mean I would start dating him. So for the next couple of months, he continued to come to the cafe whenever I worked. Which was usually five to six nights a week. I was exhausted, but I had to make sure I had enough money saved up for when I had the baby. I knew I wouldn't be able to work for at least a month, maybe more. I needed to be able to pay my bills and I would need help with the baby. Even with all my preparations, I still didn't know how I was going to do it.

I thought about calling Cormac Neeson, the President of the Cimaruta MC, Galway. But after Francesco left me, it felt wrong to accept help from the club. Even though they had been helping me since my parents passed away. After things ended with Francesco, I tried to return the money that Cormac sent to me every month. When he asked me why, I told him that we had ended things and it didn't seem right to keep taking money from the club. He told me that the help was because I had lost my parents at such a young age and because my father was part of the MC family. Which meant that I was part of the family. It wasn't because of my relationship with Francesco. So I agreed to continue to accept the money, and if I'm being honest? I don't know where I'd be without it. And now with the baby coming? I needed the money more than ever.

I knew I had to tell Cormac about the baby. It took me a little while but I finally got up the courage to call him and ask him to meet me. When I told him about the baby, I asked him not to tell Francesco. I said that he left me and didn't want anything to do with me. Which was sort of true. I mean, I never tried to contact him, but he never tried either. Cormac agreed to not tell Francesco, but asked that I didn't come around the clubhouse because the guys would ask questions. If I needed anything, I was to call him directly and he would come to me. If that was the only way I could keep this from Francesco, I would do it. But I miss my MC family so much.

It's been almost five years since then and my life has been pretty good. Callum and I have had a good relationship. But lately all I can think about is Francesco and whether or not I made the right decision about keeping the baby from him. Callum has never told me I shouldn't tell him, all he says is that I need to do what's best for me and the baby. Maybe I should contact Francesco and tell him about his daughter. But that thought terrifies me.

Chapter Two

Francesco

My twin and I were raised to be strong and protective of our mam, sisters and everyone in our family. Blood and chosen. When we turned sixteen, we had trackers hidden in our arms, as did our younger twin sisters. We did this because of the changes that were being made within our club and the possible repercussions.

When Luciana was taken and the tracking program I created almost failed, I swore it would never happen again. Because of that, I decided it was time to go to college. I wanted to learn how to make the things we needed the right way and to fix the ones that weren't working. Being self taught is great, but there are some things you need to learn from people that know more than you. Sebastiano Mancini is one of those people.

He is the head of IT for his family's company, Mancini Legacy Enterprises. He and I have been working together to make the tracking program work the way I envisioned.

It's funny how life has a way of throwing you curveballs that can make your head spin. Just when it seemed like my life was going to mellow out, *she* came back into my life.

Maeve Ciara Flanagan.

The one girl I thought I would never see again. We met in Ireland when we were fourteen. Her papà, Ansel 'Cruach' Flanagan, was the road captain for our Cimaruta MC, Galway chapter. He was one of the original members of our Galway chapter. He and his wife passed away in a motorcycle accident when we were sixteen. Maeve went to live with her nana after that, and my granda made sure the Galway club helped take care of her.

Maeve and I spent almost all of my time in Ireland together, as much as our families would allow. Our last visit was when Celestino and I were eighteen. Things were getting busier with Magic Nights, and I started to feel overwhelmed. We tried to keep the relationship going, but it was just too hard. Especially with her in Ireland and me in Chicago.

Maeve was my first for everything. Kiss. Love. Sex. And heartbreak. Since then, no one has ever come close to making me feel what I felt for her. Part of it could be because I never really let anyone in after I ended things. She's the only person who knows everything about me. Even with the club—that's the part of me that I can only talk about with my family. But since her papà was a part of our club, she knew the life. I never had to hide anything from her.

I don't know when I decided to end things. I'm not sure I really made a conscious decision to end it. I let myself get consumed with what I had going on at home. And in doing that, I lost the love of my life. There was also the allure of the women who came to the shows. I let them pull me away from the one woman who always held my heart. Now that I think back on it, I have no one to blame but myself. I never cheated on her, but I'm sure she wonders if I did. And I can't blame her for that. I haven't been back to Ireland since the last time I saw Maeve when I was eighteen. I wonder if we'll run into her while here. But really, what are the odds that I would see her? Slim to none.

After the proposal, we spend some time walking around the Cliffs of Moher. There's a shop and a cafe here. My mam says that she'd like a snack, so we head towards the cafe. And there she is. Ho-ly fuck.

My Maeve.

I see her through the cafe window and it's like all the air is sucked out of my lungs. She looks the same as the last time I saw her. Maybe a little more mature and that body I loved so much? It's even sexier than I remember. Fuck. She's still the most beautiful woman I've ever seen. My heart beats faster as I watch her work. When she finally turns and looks at me, I see the recognition in her eyes. She knows it's me.

I head inside the cafe to talk to my Maeve. At this point, I'm not even sure if anyone is following me, but it doesn't matter. My heart is screaming for her and my feet are taking me there.

"Piccola lontra." Little otter. My pet name for her rolling off my tongue like no time has passed.

Her eyes get bigger.

"F-Francesco," she says in her Irish accent that I missed so much. It's a good thing there's no line behind me because this is going to take a while.

"Can you take a break?" I ask her.

She frowns at me. Okay, I think she might still be mad at me. I mean, I don't blame her, but I was hoping she wouldn't be. It's been five years, surely that's enough time for her to stop being mad, right?

"What are you doing here?" she asks.

"Luciana just got engaged. Everyone's here for it. Mam said she wanted a snack so we were coming to the cafe. I saw you through that window." I say, pointing to the big glass window that showcases the view of the cliffs.

"Please congratulate Luciana for me."

I notice she still hasn't answered my question.

"Break, piccola lontra. When is your break?"

"Why?" she frowns again. "Don't call me that."

"Because I want to talk to you. And it's not a conversation I want to have in the middle of the cafe." Now it's my turn to ignore her request.

"I don't think there's anything that needs to be said."

My Maeve. She's still feisty after all these years. I always loved her accent. Seeing her and hearing her speak takes me back to those feelings I had when I was fourteen and I heard her speak for the first time. I fucked up by letting her go. But I'm going to fix that right now.

Then I start to panic. What if she's seeing someone? She could be married and have babies with this person. Could I really be too late?

"Please, Maeve. Can we talk during your break? There's so much I want to say."

She shakes her head. "No. I don't think we can. We should leave things the way they are."

Her voice is trembling as she speaks. It makes me want to jump over the counter and take her in my arms. There's so much more I want to say to her. But there are customers walking in and she's turned away from me to help them.

I take a seat at a table by the window to wait for her. I'm not going to leave until we talk. After what feels like years have passed, it's finally slowing down in the cafe. I watch Maeve as she moves around to clean up the counters. She's ignoring me.

I stand up and head over to her again. Right as I'm about to explain why we need to talk, a man walks out the kitchen door behind her. He hugs her, saying good morning. He calls her '*hen*'. That's an endearment that's usually used between people that know each other well. This is not fucking happening. The way he's got his arm around her, and that one word—I don't think he's just a co-worker. And she's smiling up at him. Oh, fuck no. She's *mine*.

He whispers something to her, and she responds by whispering something back. Then they both turn and look at me. I frown and cross my arms over my chest. He's smaller than me, but that won't stop me from ripping his arms off.

"Are you able to take your break now?" I ask Maeve.

"I told you we have nothing to talk about, Francesco."

"We have a lot to talk about. Please. Just give me a chance to explain things."

"You need to leave. Maeve said she doesn't want to talk to you." He has a Scottish accent, and that pisses me off even more. I don't even know why—but everything about him pisses me off.

"This doesn't involve you."

"If it involves Maeve, it involves me."

Oh, fuck no. Is that his way of staking his claim on

my woman? Fuck that. This asshole needs to leave now if he wants to keep his pretty face looking pretty.

Maeve puts her hand on his chest. "I'm going to take my break."

He starts to protest, but I step in and glare at him.

"Back off," I growl. "I don't know who you are, but Maeve and I need to talk."

She finally nods at me and sighs. "Fine. Let's go out back. We can have some privacy out there."

I follow her out the back door. There are a few picnic tables overlooking the cliffs. I love it here. This is where I'm going to win my girl back.

She sits down on one of the benches. "What do you want to talk about, Francesco?"

Taking a seat next to her, I take her hands in mine. To my surprise, she doesn't pull away. But she won't look at me, she keeps staring at our hands. My heart feels like it's going to beat out of my chest.

"First, I want to say how sorry I am for the way things ended. I was a stupid kid. Can you forgive me?"

Maeve

Francesco Liam Bastianini.

He didn't just break my heart, he kicked it around and stomped on it. We met when we were fourteen years old and spent four amazing years together. It wasn't easy, but we made it work. He lived in Chicago and I lived in Galway. But with phone calls, texts and letters, we found a way to keep it going. He visited me in Ireland with his family and I got to visit him in Chicago. I thought we would get married and have a family. We talked about our future often.

Then the calls started getting shorter and farther between. Then the texts went from several times a day to once, maybe twice a day. Then the letters stopped coming. We wrote to each other once a week—for all four years. Then one week there wasn't one. I tried not to be hurt by it. His reason for not writing was that he had a hard week and he would make it up to me with the next letter. So I wrote mine like I always did. I never got another letter from him. Or a phone call. Everything just stopped.

A month later, I got a text. It said that he didn't realize how hard it would be getting the business up and running. That he loved me, but he didn't want me to wait for him to figure things out, and it wasn't fair to me. Coward. That wasn't easier for me, it was easier for *him*. I saw the videos they posted of their shows. When he started dancing, I never worried about the women or that he was almost naked in front of them. I was secure in my knowledge of how much he loved me and how solid we were as a couple. I would've continued to trust him forever. But after the way he left me? You're damn right, I wondered. Was I that much of an *eejit* that I didn't see what he was doing? All those women throwing themselves at him...

FOUR feckin' years! I hated him so much for such

a long time. I had given him everything. My heart, my body, my time...and that was how he chose to end things. In a text. That eejit didn't even have the balls to call me or even wait till we were face to face.

Now, five years later, he's here. On *my* island. I want to hate him, tell him to fuck off and stay away from me. But I find myself telling him I forgive him. What the hell is going on?

"You broke my heart, Francesco, but yes, I forgive you. It took me a long time to climb out of that dark place you put me in when you disappeared. But I forgive you for the way you handled things."

What the fuck am I saying? Why am I forgiving the bastard? There's so much more I want to say, but before I can, his lips are on mine. And it's like the last five years never happened. How does he do that?

I pull back from the kiss to look into his beautiful blue-green eyes. The eyes that I loved so much. Loved. Who am I kidding? Love. I still love Francesco Bastianini. I never stopped. I'm so screwed.

"You're still as beautiful as the last time I saw you. Please give me another chance. You've always been my everything," he whispers, not taking his eyes off of me.

This can't be real. When he left me, I didn't know how to keep going, but somehow I did. Then finding out I was pregnant made my world spin. But now he's back. Saying all the things I wished he had said to me back then. My heart is screaming *yes*. My head is whispering *no*. But my traitorous body is saying *feck, yes*. Let's just say I can't trust my body around Franco.

I've never had any self-control with him. It doesn't seem like it's going to be any different this time.

"Are you with someone? That schmuck you work with?" He frowns.

He sounds angry. Did he really think I stayed single this whole time? And what's a 'schmuck'? I frown and shake myself. Callum. How could I have forgotten about Callum? Francesco comes back and I somehow forget everything that's happened the last five years.

"Callum and I have been together for four years," I say.

Francesco was always possessive. Alpha to his core, he's even growled at a few men for looking at me. I can see that part of him surfacing and if I'm being honest, I've always loved it. I watch his emotions go from passive to angry in a matter of seconds. I know he'd never physically hurt me. But I'm pretty sure he'd hurt a man for looking at me.

Francesco

What the fuck. Okay fine, I didn't expect her to be single for the last five years. Well, maybe I did. That way, I could come in and sweep her off her feet. I don't care who I have to go through to win Maeve back. But it feels like there's more that she wants to say. I can feel a knot of dread growing in my stomach. She can't have a family with that schmuck. Life wouldn't punish me that much, would it?

"Are you with him now?" I sound pathetic, practically begging Maeve to tell me what I want to hear.

She stares at me for what seems like hours. But it's probably only been like five seconds.

"Not right now."

I stare into her eyes. Did I just hear that right? And instead of being a good person and at least pretending that I understand her sadness, I say, "Good. He doesn't deserve you."

As soon as those words are out of my mouth, I regret them. But before I can take it back, my girl scrunches up her face.

"How would you know? You left me with no explanation," she spits out, poking her finger at my chest. "You don't even know Callum, he's been here for me through everything..." she trails off.

I know she's holding something back. I need to know what it is. I fucked up before. But I'm going to make it right.

"Talk to me, Maeve. Please."

We need more time, but I see my family approaching. When they get to us, they all hug Maeve. There goes our talking time. It's okay, though. Watching all of them together makes my heart happy. It's like the last five years never happened. She's still a part of our family and always will be.

"How long are you in Ireland for?" she asks everyone.

"Two weeks, maybe three," my sister Luciana answers. "We should all have dinner and hang out."

Maeve nods. "That would be really nice."

They exchange numbers.

"I need to get back inside," Maeve says.

"What time do you get off?" I ask her.

"Not till five."

"Can I pick you up? Take you for a bite to eat?" I blurt out. I can't let her get away.

"I'm sorry, I can't tonight, Francesco."

I try not to frown at her, because no matter how much I need to be with her, that doesn't mean she's feeling the same way. And it doesn't escape me that she keeps calling me 'Francesco.' That's something she always did when she was angry with me.

"Do you work tomorrow?"

She lets out a small sigh. "I agree, we do need to talk. I'll text you tonight after I get home."

I want to keep pushing her, but I don't know how much more she can take. So I back off a little.

"Ok, but you promise to text me tonight?"

I still sound so fucking pathetic. And you know what? I don't care. Maeve is the only woman I've ever loved. And I'm not going to let her go this time.

"I promise," she answers. Then she turns and heads back inside the cafe. It takes everything in me not to follow her. Instead, I let Luciana take my hand and take me back to our group.

Chapter Three

Maeve

"So that's Francesco Bastianini?" Callum asks as I walk back into the cafe. He doesn't sound angry, he sounds sad. Like he knows this isn't going to end the way he wants. I know he was watching us while we talked. When Francesco left me, I thought I would never find anyone else. Callum showed me that I was worthy of being loved. But I've never loved him the way I loved Francesco. I think that's something he's always known. My heart will never be his, not in the way it should be if we're going to spend the rest of our lives together. I feel horrible admitting that, even if it's only to myself. If there was a way to make it better, I would. But facts are facts, and there's no changing it.

It's been four and a half years since the day Callum walked into my life. He's been my best friend and lover. Two weeks ago, we decided to take a break. These last few months, I've been feeling like I'm being unfair to him. There's always been a part of my heart that was waiting for Francesco to come back. Even though I never really thought he would. Callum and I live together, but have been sleeping in different rooms since we separated. I wish I knew the right thing to do. Callum said he always knew how I felt. That there's a part of me that'll never be his. He doesn't like it, but he loves me enough to accept it.

And there's the secret I'm hiding from Francesco. It's a big one. I don't know if he'll ever forgive me for keeping this from him. There's no going back now—no regrets, right? Tell that to my racing heart. I don't know why it even matters if he's pissed at me or not. We're not together now and we'll never be together again.

Taking a deep breath, I turn to Callum. "Yes, that's Francesco."

The look on his face kills me. I know it's hurting him just knowing that Francesco is here in Ireland. He could deal with my feelings when Francesco was in Chicago, but now that he's here? It changes everything.

Callum reaches out to hold me. "I love you, Maeve. More than I could ever express in words. I've always known that I wasn't the love of your life. But I hoped in time that could change."

Hearing him say that makes me sad. He's done

nothing but love me and this is how I make him feel? Like he isn't enough for me. I never wanted him to feel like that.

"I love you too, Callum. You saved me when I thought I couldn't be saved. You helped me through one of the worst times in my life."

"Are you going back to him?" he asks. His voice sounds broken. But he deserves nothing less than the truth.

"I don't know what I'm going to do. There's a lot we need to talk about. I've kept this secret from him for so long. I don't think he'll be able to get past that."

"If he doesn't understand why you kept this from him, then he's a bigger eejit than I originally thought. And he doesn't deserve you."

"Why are you so good to me?" It's taking everything in me not to break down right here in the cafe.

"You're everything to me, Maeve. You gave me a family, showed me what it means to be a part of something bigger than just me. It kills me to know that I could lose you to him. But even if you choose him, that won't change how I feel about you."

I don't know what to do. My heart says I need to give Francesco the chance to explain. Yet there's a part of me that wants to stay with Callum. He's never hurt me. Never made me feel second best to anyone or anything. Never given up on me. Francesco has done all of that.

Maybe that's why I kept this secret from him. Because I knew it was the one thing that I could have that he couldn't. If I told him and let him back in, he could hurt me again.

But now I have no choice. It's time. I've always believed in fate and him being here is fate telling me to make things right.

Francesco

I watch that fucker put his arms around my Maeve. Before I can go in and rip them off, my twin is beside me, forcing me away from the window.

"Don't do it, Franco. That's not how you're going to win her back," Celestino says to me.

I know he's right, but fuck if I care. She's mine and he's touching her. So again I feel myself veering towards the cafe. And again, there's my twin, pulling me back.

"Let her come to you. If she doesn't text you, I'll come back with you tomorrow."

"I fucked up, Tino. Me. I need her to understand how fucking sorry I am."

"I know you do. But going in there and demanding that of her is not the way. Let her have some say in this. You know you fucked up and hurt her. I saw the look in her eyes. She'll come to you."

"How can you be so sure? What if she doesn't?"

How much of a baby do I sound like? Big bad biker reduced to a pile of blubbering goo because of a woman. No. Because of THE woman. The only woman who has ever had control of my heart. The one I never thought would come back into my life again. I'm fucking doomed.

That look on Maeve's face before she went back in —she said we needed to talk more. What is it that she needs to say? It feels like something huge. No matter what it is, we'll get through it together. I'm not letting her go a second time. The first time almost killed me. The second time definitely will.

Maeve

When the whole family came back for lunch, they all sat outside on the picnic tables. I got to see his parents and grandparents. I really missed them. I also met Luciana's fiancé, Rónán, and his family. His parents made me promise to come to the islands to visit.

What I need to talk to Francesco about is making me nauseous. I feel like a horrible person for keeping this from him.

"It's going to be okay, hen," Callum says softly. "No matter what happens, I'll always be here for you. For both of you."

I hug him tight. "Thank you, Callum, I know this

can't be easy for you. I appreciate everything you do for us."

"Let's finish cleaning up and go home. We have things to discuss too."

I nod as we work together in our comfortable silence, cleaning up and restocking. We both have the day off tomorrow. Maybe I can avoid seeing Francesco while he's here. Luciana said they're here for two weeks, maybe three. I can take that time off and not come into work. Callum owns the cafe now, and I know he wouldn't say no to that. Especially if it means that I'll stay away from Francesco.

But hiding is how I got into this position. So I know that's not the solution. I need to be an adult and finally own up to my part in this.

Walking into the house I share with Callum makes me feel like I'm doing something wrong. Because I can't stop thinking about Francesco. If he hadn't walked into the cafe today, I could've spent the rest of my life with Callum, even with our separation. But now? I don't know what to do. I don't want to hurt Callum; he doesn't deserve it in the least.

When I met Callum, I was about five months pregnant. He would come into the cafe I worked in every night. The wounds that Francesco left me with were fresh, and I wasn't looking to be with anyone. Somehow, without me even knowing, he became a part of my nightly routine. Callum never pushed or judged me for the situation I was in. He just listened and made me feel like I was safe, something I needed after what happened with Francesco.

I went into labor one night while I was on shift—it was unexpected because I wasn't due for three more weeks. Callum was there as usual and drove me to the hospital. When they asked if he was the father, he told them he was and I wasn't in the right headspace to say no. Truthfully, I didn't want to do it alone. I gave birth to a little girl, I named her Saoirse. She's been such a blessing in my life.

"I'm going to pick up Saoirse and take her to get a snack. That will give you time to text Francesco."

It's killing me to hear the hurt in his voice. I get up and hug him tight. He's been my rock, my savior, all these years. I wish I could tell him that I choose him and that I can let Francesco go. But I just can't get myself to say it. And the look in his eyes tells me he knows.

"Thank you."

He gives me a kiss on the cheek and hugs me. I watch him pull out of our driveway. I'm a horrible person for doing this to him. And my baby, she thinks Callum's her da. What's going to happen when I tell Francesco? No, I know what's going to happen. He's going to demand to see her and be in her life. And where does that leave Callum? I can't expect him to just walk away. I need Francesco to understand that Saoirse needs Callum too.

Maybe I won't mention her just yet. I've kept this secret for this long...

A little longer won't hurt, right?

Francesco

I've never really been a patient man, and right now the tiny sliver I had left has disappeared completely. Waiting for Maeve to reach out to me is like being the frog in the pot of water. You know the metaphor of the frog? The one that's sitting in a pot of water that's slowly coming to a full boil. Yet the frog is just lounging in the water because it's oblivious to what's coming.

"Let's get some dinner," Keegan suggests. He's the oldest of the O'Callaghan brothers.

Celestino hauls me up and gets me moving. "Stop being pathetic. She'll text when she's ready."

I know he's right, but I just can't get myself to relax. Looking around at everyone, I sigh. Our parents and grandparents have gone out shopping. I'm glad they're not here to see the mess I've become. It's bad enough that my siblings are here for this.

I sigh again and follow them out to the car. We drive to the heart of Galway and park. Quay street is a quaint area with tons of shops and pubs. I start to relax as we walk around; I think I even smile and laugh a little.

While we're looking for a pub we all like, I see the guy that Maeve is with. Callum. He sees me at the same time and tries to duck into an ice cream shop called Gino's. But not before I see him holding the hand of a little girl.

Maeve has a child?

My heart stops as I look at the little girl. She looks just like Luciana did when she was a kid.

As we walk by the shop, I try to get another look at the little girl. She can't be mine...can she? FUCK. Did I hurt Maeve so much that she would keep my baby from me?

"What's wrong, Franco?" my sister Bella asks as she bumps into me.

"I just saw the guy Maeve is with. He had a little girl with him," I say, my eyes glued to the ice cream shop's front door.

"Wait. You think she's Maeve's kid? Maybe she's his kid and not hers?" She's looking at the door with me.

"The little girl looks like Luciana." I hear her gasp beside me.

I think I have a daughter. And Maeve said nothing to me. Not. One. Word. I'm not sure I can put all the blame on her...I'm the one who left her. Maybe she felt like she couldn't tell me? Ah, fuck that. If that's my daughter, I've missed out on five years of knowing her.

"I'm going in there." I barely hear Luciana before I see her barreling towards the ice cream shop. I reach out to grab her.

"Don't."

"Why? This is huge, Franco!" she growls at me.

"Let me talk to Maeve first. If she's mine, going in there and making a scene won't do any good. She's a little girl, I don't want her first memory of me to be fear."

Luciana huffs out a breath and nods at me. I love my sisters and have no doubt they have my back. But I also don't want this little girl to fear any of us.

Chapter Four

Maeve

I'm trying to get up the courage to text Francesco. But my hands won't stop shaking. Taking a deep breath, I pull up his number and stare at the blank screen. Right as I'm about to type, I get a text from Callum.

> Callum: I just saw Francesco. He's here on Quay

> Maeve: Did he see you and Saoirse?

> Callum: I'm pretty sure he did. I'm sorry. I took her into Gino's, he didn't follow us. But I can see him and the others watching the door, he's still out there

Maeve: It's okay, if he tries to talk to you, please don't say anything about Saoirse. I need to tell him about her myself

Callum: I know, hen. I won't say anything. I'm waiting for them to move on and then we'll head home. The longer we stay here, the bigger the chance he'll come and find us

Maeve: Okay, thank you. Drive safe

Callum: Always

Dammit.

So now the question is, do I text Francesco or not? Is it finally time to tell him about Saoirse? I'm afraid that he might want to take her from me. He has more money than I do and better resources. All I have is my love for my little girl. My little girl with her blue-green eyes...Francesco's eyes.

Francesco: Is she mine?

That one text sends me running to the bathroom, and I dry heave for a few minutes. He did see them. How do I explain this to him? I kept his daughter a secret these last five years. I sit on the floor in my bathroom and stare at his text.

I know he would've come back to me if I had told him. But I never wanted him to be with me out of obligation. Maybe that's enough for some people, but

I'm not one of them. I always dreamed of a love like my parents had. My da was a rough biker, the road captain for the Cimaruta MC, but with my mam? He was loyal, protective, soft and kind. They loved each other with everything they had. I miss them both so much. I wish they were here, they'd know exactly what I should do. Before Francesco left me, I thought I had found what my parents had. I wish I had been right.

> Francesco: Please, Maeve. Talk to me.
> I saw her with Callum…she looks like
> Luciana when she was little

I don't know when the tears started, but my eyes have turned into waterfalls. I knew this day would come. But I thought I would have more time to figure out how to tell him. A part of me hoped that she would be older when the time came.

Time to put my big girl pants on and figure out how to tell him about Saoirse. And explain why I didn't tell him five years ago. I could say it's all his fault because of the way he left me. But that's the coward's way and I'm no coward.

> Maeve: Where are you?

Playing dumb could buy me some time. My hands are shaking so bad as I type.

Francesco: I'm in town, we're looking
for a place to eat. You didn't answer
my question…

Maeve: Are you busy tomorrow? We
can meet up and talk

Francesco: I always have time for you.
What time and where?

Maeve: Salthill beach? Around eleven?

Francesco: Okay, I'll see you there

Telling him about Saoirse is not something I can do in a text. Not that it'll be any easier to tell him in person. I just hope he understands why I did what I did. I ask myself, would I be understanding about something like this? Probably not.

My stomach is still in knots an hour later when Callum and Saoirse walk in the door.

"Mam!" Saoirse yells as she comes running to me. "Da took me to get ice cream. We brought you some too!"

I hold my little girl tight and breathe her in.

"Thank you, baby."

"Squishing me, mam." She giggles.

"Why don't you get ready to take a bath. I'll be there to start your water soon."

"Okay, Mam."

I watch her run down the hallway and into her room. We can hear her greeting each of her stuffed animals, something she does every day, and I love it.

"Are you ok?" Callum asks as he's putting the ice cream away. Then he comes to me and hugs me.

"I'm scared. What if he tries to take her from me?"

Callum lets out a growl. "I'll never let him take her. I'll give my last euro to keep her with you. Don't you worry, hen."

I can't help the sob that escapes me. We stand there for a few minutes while Callum rubs my back. He's always had this way to make me feel okay with my decisions. And his protective side rivals Francesco's.

"I want you to know something. Please look at me, Maeve."

I sniffle and raise my eyes to look into his grey ones.

"No matter what you choose to do, I'll always be here for you. If I thought I could keep you with me by force, I would. But I know that I can't do that. You and Saoirse are my world and I will protect you both with my last breath. He better be worth your love. Both of you. I only ask that you let me continue to be in her life. I know she'll learn that I'm not her real da. But that doesn't mean I don't love her like she's mine."

I can't promise Callum that he's the one I'll choose. But I can promise that I won't take Saoirse from him. He deserves to be in her life. Francesco might be jealous at the beginning, but I know he'll understand.

"I would never exclude you from Saoirse's life. She loves you so much. The only way that could happen is if you—"

"That'll never happen," he says before I can finish

my sentence. "Even if you choose to be with Francesco, Saoirse will always be mine too."

I don't know what I did to deserve having Callum in my life. But I'm forever grateful that he is. He appeared when I needed someone and I know that one day he will find his person. Because I've always known that Francesco was mine.

Francesco

Maeve still hasn't answered my question about the little girl I saw with Callum. I watched them leave the ice cream shop. She's a beautiful little girl. I'm pretty sure she's mine, but I heard her call Callum 'Da.' I wish I knew why Maeve kept her from me. Was she that angry? Who am I kidding, of course she was angry. But to keep my child from me? I don't know if I can accept that. I know I'm getting ahead of myself and I can't get my thoughts straight. Maybe she isn't mine, but if she's not, wouldn't Maeve just come out and say that? Fuck.

"What are you going to do?" Luciana asks.

"I don't know, Maeve won't say if she's mine. But you saw her, she has to be a Bastianini. Right?"

Luciana nods at me. "She looks like me when I was little. If you find out that she's yours and Maeve has kept her from you all these years...can you forgive her? Would you still want to be with her?"

"Can I forgive her? I think so. I never stopped

loving her. She's always had my heart, that hasn't changed. Do I understand why she would keep this from me? No. I'll also be talking to the Ireland chapter about this. They had to have known and not one of those assholes told us."

Luciana looks at me. "If so, it wasn't their place to tell you, Franco."

"They're our brothers. FAMILY. Someone in the chapter should've told me I have a daughter. I need to find a way to understand why she did this. The only thing I do know is that we will find our way back to each other."

"I'm always behind you, big brother. If Maeve is who you choose, I'll welcome her back into the family. But if she hurts you? I won't be so understanding. Even if you ask me to be."

I hug my sister tight. Our family has always been the center of our lives. This situation makes that even more important to me. Because I know they'll all back me up, no matter what I decide to do. In time, they'll forgive Maeve for not telling me I had a daughter.

My heart is pulling me to Maeve. But my head is saying not to give in so fast. My body? It didn't get the memo that she's mad at us. I've been uncomfortable since the moment I saw her. But how do I choose which way to go? The last time I listened to my head, I lost the love of my life. I can't make that same mistake again.

If that little girl is mine, I've lost five years with her. Then again, Callum could be her papà. How will I win Maeve back if she's not mine?

I should never have left her in the first place. I wouldn't be in this position if I had been smarter back then. But I was a boy, not a man, and I made a decision a boy would make. I'm no longer that boy.

Tomorrow can't come fast enough. Why is it that when you want time to speed up, it feels like it's dragging on? Right now, it feels like tomorrow is years away.

"I'm meeting Maeve tomorrow," I say to my brother.

"How do you feel about it?" he asks.

"Honestly? Part of me is excited to see her and get some answers. But I'm still pissed she kept this from me for so long. If we hadn't seen her at the cafe, would she ever have told me?"

"I wish I knew, little brother. But she might not have those answers for you. You were both young and the way you left her...well it wasn't pretty."

"Fuck. I know, Tino. I've kicked myself every day since I cut things off with her. I can't even tell you why I did it."

"Come on Franco, you know why. There were girls hitting on us constantly. I mean, that hasn't changed, but we're older now and we know those women aren't what we want. Admit it."

I hate my twin. Why does he have to know me so damn well? Admitting to Maeve that the women were like catnip to a cat is like telling her that she didn't matter to me. And that's not true. Not even a little. I was eighteen and had women throwing money and their bodies at me. I should've been a better, stronger person. Instead, I was a weak asshole. But I never cheated on her. Not once.

Even though I'm angry about her secret, I put her in that position. I need to remember that tomorrow. We did this to each other.

We finally find a cafe that will hold all of us and sit down to eat. Sitting here watching my family is making me sad. If Saoirse is mine, she's missed out on being a part of us. I have a lot to make up to her and Maeve. There's a pit in my stomach when I think about how alone she must have felt.

Falling asleep is proving to be just as hard as it was to not text Maeve. It's taking a lot of restraint to be patient. There's that part of me that wants to push her to tell me, and then I can start to take care of them. I know she probably doesn't need me to, but I'm going to do it, anyway. I'm sure Maeve knows this about me. I've missed holding her, I can still remember how it felt to fall asleep with her in my arms.

Tomorrow can't come fast enough.

Chapter Five

Maeve

Waking up this morning, I feel sick. On one hand, there's Callum, and on the other is the love of my life. You would think that this decision would be easy. Love of your life overrides all others, right? Wrong. What if that love of your life hurt you so much, the pain is still fresh five years later? I want to believe Francesco when he says that he wants me. But he said that before. He told me I was his everything and that we would spend the rest of our lives together. Then one day he left me. And all the dreams I had for my future went with him. Until Callum. When I finally saw him clearly, I realized that I still owned part of my heart and I gave it to Callum.

So how do I walk away from the person who saved

me? Does true love really trump every other kind of love? Maybe. I just don't know.

What I do know is that I have to meet with Francesco today. I have to tell him about my daughter—his daughter. Our daughter. My beautiful Saoirse. I see so much of Francesco in her. Not only in the color of her eyes, she has his personality. She's always standing up for other kids that are being bullied. She's only four years old, yet she has such an old soul. Just like my Francesco.

As I'm staring into my closet trying to decide what to wear, I feel Callum's arms slide their way around my body. I lean back into him and sigh.

"I'll keep Saoirse today. You and Francesco need to talk and I don't think that her being there will be good for her. I already called the school to let them know she'd be staying home today."

This. This is a big reason why I love Callum. He always thinks of what's best for Saoirse. He's never once treated her like she wasn't his. From the first day she came into this world, he has always protected her.

I look in on Saoirse before I head out.

"I'll call you after I see Francesco. I'm sorry that I'm putting you through this," I whisper.

"This is not your fault."

"I feel like it is. It's because I was a coward and never told him about Saoirse. That's why we're here now."

"Marry me. We have a good life together. I love you and Saoirse."

"D-Did you just ask me to marry you?"

"Aye, hen. Marry me."

"Callum...I-I don't know. I need time to think about it. You know I love you...but I need to sort things out with Francesco before I can think about the future. I'm so sorry."

Seeing the fallen look on his face is killing me. I don't want to say 'no' right now. Because I know that we could have a wonderful life together. But Francesco. My heart is crying out to let him know about Saoirse before I make a decision.

Callum steps back and looks at me.

"I understand, hen, but I want you to know I'm serious about my proposal. But I also know you need to talk to Francesco and figure out where the two of you stand with each other. You'll figure all this out," he says.

I step forward and wrap my arms around him, hugging him tight. I wish I could accept Callum's proposal.

Francesco

It's finally time, and I'm trying to figure out how to meet Maeve without everyone following me. I don't think I'm going to be able to do that.

"What time are we leaving to meet Maeve?" Isabella asks me.

"We?" I laugh.

"Yes, 'we.'" She rolls her eyes at me.

"I can't have all of you there when I meet her. She's already nervous and that would just make it worse."

Isabella is staring at me like I've gone crazy. I'm not crazy, I just know how my family is, and they can be intimidating. Even for those that know them.

"Fine. But when we get there, you need to promise to let me handle it. I fucked it up five years ago and now it's up to me to fix things."

Luciana makes a noise that sounds like a snort. It definitely didn't sound like a yes.

"The hell it's your fault. What you did back then? Yes. That's your fault, you were a shitbag. But to keep your daughter from you all these years? To me, that's worse."

"Come on Ana, are you saying that if it was you and Rónán in this situation, that you wouldn't do what Maeve did?"

"Fuck no. That's not what I'm saying. I would've made him suffer from the moment he stepped back into my life."

She smiles that sweet, yet evil, smile. She can be a little devil sometimes, I think that comes with being the youngest of four. And now I know she's not going to hold back with Maeve. Fuck.

"But I wouldn't have kept his child from him. No matter how angry I was, he'd still deserve to know his child. That's the part I'm having trouble with. It's not like she didn't know how to get in touch with you. She *chose* not to tell you."

That's the hardest thing to understand. But in an hour, I'll have some answers. At least I hope I will.

"We need to leave in fifteen minutes," I tell everyone.

"Everything will be okay, Son. Maeve had her reasons for doing what she did. Even if you don't agree with them, you have to remember she thought she was doing what was right for her and the child. Sometimes things can get out of hand, and by the time you realize it, you feel like it's impossible go back and fix it." My mam is one of the best women I know. Her advice has never taken me down the wrong path. I remember when I ended things with Maeve, my mam was so angry at me for the way I handled it. She said I should've talked to her before I just walked away. I wish I had done that.

This time, I'm going to make sure I remember what she said. Remember that maybe, just maybe, Maeve felt she had no other choice than to keep this from me. But my club? They have no fucking excuse. One of the council members should've told me. We see them at least twice a year and talk weekly.

"I want to go to the clubhouse first. Those bastards are going to explain themselves."

"If you have to, I'm coming with you. I am the president and whether you like it or not, your sister is right. It wasn't their place to tell you. You never asked them about Maeve, so maybe they thought you didn't care. We don't know their reasons. But you will not go in there, guns blazing. You don't get to blame them for this."

I scowl at my papà. It doesn't matter if he's right; I need to go and find out why they didn't tell me. Fine. I fucking admit it—it wasn't their place. But in our world, we're family. And you're supposed to be able to rely on your family in any situation. No matter who's involved.

"Are you listening to me, Francesco?" my papà snaps at me.

"I heard you, papà. I just want to know why. And if they say it's cause I never asked? Well then, that's on me. But they should've told me anyway. What if they were in this situation? I can guarantee they would've wanted to know."

"I get it, Franco, I truly do. She kept this from all of us, not just you. But you can't go back and change it, so blaming the club isn't the answer. You need to work through this with Maeve."

I nod at my papà, I know my parents are right. But I still need to talk to the club.

While we're driving to the clubhouse, I call Cormac 'Chainsaw' Neeson—president of the Galway,

Ireland chapter. When my granda stepped down as president, he appointed Chainsaw as his successor. My granda gave Cormac the road name 'Chainsaw' because the day he became a prospect, they had him cutting wood for winter. Granda said he never once complained and kept at it for a whole week.

I let Chainsaw know we're all on our way to the clubhouse and that I wanted to talk to him. He wanted to know why, but I'm not going to get into it on the phone.

When we get to the clubhouse, I head straight inside. There are some guys lounging around and a few bunnies hanging onto them. Some things never change. Bunnies are like groupies, but for the club instead of a band. They're not allowed to live on the property, but they are 'property' of the club in the sense that they don't hang around other MCs. The way they earn their protection is to keep the clubhouse clean, cook for the brothers, and take care of them sexually, if that's what the brothers want. No one is forced to be here, and they know what the deal is before they ask if they can hang around with the club. This in no way means that they're a part of the club. The bunnies used to be called 'sweet butts', but my sisters made comments a while back about how the women bounce around and sleep with any of the brothers. So they started calling them bunnies instead.

Chainsaw greets us the minute we walk in, and we each give him a hug.

"Did you want to talk privately?" he asks me.

"Away from nosy ears? Yes," I answer. We follow him into the room where they hold church, and everyone sits down.

"How's the trip been so far?" he asks us.

"It's been good, Fuoco finally suckered a guy into marrying her," Giustizia teases.

Fuoco slowly gets up, walks over to Giustizia and punches him in the arm. Then casually walks back to her chair and sits back down. My papà is chuckling and shaking his head.

"It's good to see some things never change." Chainsaw laughs, then turns to me. "You sounded serious when you called earlier. Is something going on?"

"Did you know Maeve Flanagan had a baby?"

His head drops, and he lets out a big sigh. "I knew. She begged me not to tell you. Said that you left her and didn't want her or the baby. I didn't want to believe her, but she seemed so sincere. And when you never asked about her, I thought maybe she was telling the truth."

"So you know for a fact that the girl is mine? I saw her yesterday with that guy, Callum. She called him 'Da'.'"

"You should talk to Maeve. You're my brother, but this is something you need to work out between the two of you."

All I want to do right now is punch Chainsaw in the face. But he's fucking right. This is between Maeve and me.

"I plan on talking to her after we leave here. But I

wanted to know how much the club knew. And why no one thought of telling me she had a kid."

"Again, brother, I did what I thought was best for her. What Maeve's da would've wanted us to do. I've made sure she wanted for nothing. And Callum is a good man, I vetted him myself. He's treated them both well, and he's a hard worker. He owns that cafe at the Cliffs of Moher."

Well, fuck. I wanted Callum to be a piece of shit, that way I could swoop in and rescue Maeve from a horrible life. Looks like I have my work cut out for me. I just hope she still wants me.

"Thank you for taking care of them. But from now on, that will be my responsibility. They're both mine."

He studies my face and finally nods at me.

"If that's what you want. The deal I made with her was that she wouldn't come around the clubhouse. No one but me knows that the girl is hers."

"Again, thank you for everything you've done for them."

Chapter Six

Maeve

I can't stop shaking while I wait for Francesco to show up. I'm hoping he'll come alone, but I'm pretty sure he won't. I always loved that about his family, they remind me of the Three Musketeers. All for one and one for all, that's the Bastianinis. They always have each other's backs, I'm sure this time will be no different.

When I met Francesco and his siblings, I was in awe of their family. Growing up, it was just me, Mam and Da. Our family was small, but I was loved. When they died, it felt like I had lost everything. But at the time, I had Francesco and his family. They helped me through that tragedy and made me feel like I'd never be alone. In between his visits here and my trips to see him in Chicago, the club helped my grandmother take care of me.

After Francesco left me, I begged Cormac not to tell any of them about Saoirse. I explained to him that if Francesco really loved me, he never would have left me. And that this was best for the both of us. The deal was that he would keep my secret, but I had to stay away from the clubhouse. He didn't want any of the other guys to have to lie for me. There was always the chance I could run into them. But when I did, if I had Saoirse with me, I would say I was babysitting. She was too little to understand what I was really saying. I was never really sure if Cormac told any of the Bastianinis and I worried that one of them would pop up. It never happened. Cormac has kept my secret and I've stayed away from the clubhouse. He always made sure I was taken care of,. Even now, money just appears in my account every month and I know it's from him.

I see Francesco walking towards me with his siblings and their friends. When I get a text from Callum.

Callum: Grandad and Granny asked if they could take Saoirse for lunch and to the park today

Maeve: Of course. She'll love that

Callum: Aye, she will. They hinted she could stay over too. Lol

Maeve: I don't mind if you don't

Callum: Okay, hen. I'm going to drop her off in about fifteen minutes. I'll see you when you get home

Maeve: Thank you

I don't know what I would do without Callum and I hate that he's hurting right now. Thankfully, Franco's parents aren't with him today. I don't think I could deal with all of them at once. I stand up as they get closer. Luciana surprises me by coming up to me and hugging me.

"Please be honest and gentle with him, he's never stopped loving you. I know that's hard to believe, but it's the truth," she whispers in my ear as she holds on to me.

I don't trust my voice, so all I can do is nod.

"We'll be at that cafe if you need us," Celestino says to the both of us.

"Thanks," Francesco says. We watch them walk away.

He doesn't even wait for them to get to the cafe to ask, "Is she mine?"

I guess there's no easing into this. Taking a deep breath, I start to explain.

"She is, her name is Saoirse. Please don't hate me for not telling you. I was so scared when I found out and it was only a couple of months after you left me. I didn't want you to feel you had to come back to me because of the baby."

Francesco

Holy crap, she *is* mine. I mean, I know what she looks like, but to hear Maeve confirm it…

"Maeve. First, I can't apologize enough for how I handled things back then. I was an idiot. I'm sorry I made you feel like it would've been a burden to me, or that it would've forced me to come back to you. There were so many times I wanted to reach out to you since then. But I was afraid that you hated me too much and it was too late."

"I hated you for a long time. I hated that you left after telling me you never would. All the dreams we made died. But in time I got stronger, and I realized that I was something, even without you. And I wanted to tell you about her, but by then I just didn't know how."

"I talked to Cormac. He told me he kept your secret."

"Please don't blame him, I begged him not to tell you. I convinced him that you didn't want me or the baby."

Hearing the panic in her voice makes me sad. I never want Maeve to regret her choices.

"I talked to Cormac before I came here to meet you. I'm sorry that I made you feel like you couldn't tell me. If you can forgive me for the way I ended things, I can forgive you for not telling me."

"Really?" she asks. I can see the shock on her face.

"Yes. Of course it hurts that I missed five years with the both of you. But I'm as much to blame as you are. Maybe more because of the way I left you."

She grabs me and hugs me. "I never thought I'd hear you say you forgive me for not telling you."

I hug her back. "I never stopped loving you, piccola lontra. And now that I know you've given me a beautiful daughter, I don't know if I can walk away from you. Either of you."

Maeve

I never thought Francesco would forgive me so easily. I admit I'm relieved that he's willing to, though. Now the question is, what does he want? I want to believe he wants me, but I just don't know.

"Now that you know, what do you want?" My voice shakes as I get the words out.

"Want? I just told you what I want. I want you, Maeve. You and our daughter."

Wait, what?

"What do you mean? You want me and Saoirse?"

He frowns at me. "Which part is confusing for you, Maeve? I want my family. You and Saoirse are my family."

"How do you see that working? We live here in Ireland, you live in Chicago."

He stops and thinks about it. "Come and live with me in Chicago."

"I can't just pack up my life and hers to follow you home. I don't have enough savings, a job, or a place to live there."

"I will take care of you both."

He says it like it's the most natural thing in the world. Just follow him home and our family will fall into place. Well, it doesn't work like that. If I rely on him to survive, I'm leaving myself open for him to hurt me again. And if he hurts me again, where will I go?

"What if you decide being a full-time da is not what you want? Saoirse isn't a toy that can be returned when you're tired of her. And what if you decide you don't want to be with me again? Then not only do I need to figure things out for me, but for Saoirse too. She's the most important person in this scenario."

I watch his face go from relaxed to angry, and he takes a deep breath.

"I know Saoirse isn't a toy. I would never 'return her', no matter how hard it is. I get that you don't trust me right now. But I'm asking you to at least give me a chance to prove that I've changed."

"And what about your job? The women that are all over you at your shows? I don't know if I can deal with that."

"That's something we'll work on together. I don't want any of those women, I never did. I made a stupid decision that I wish I could go back and change. It's just my job. You'll see that when you come to the shows with me."

Can I really trust him? I've always wondered if he crossed any lines before he left me. And right now, I need to know that answer. I want to look into his eyes when I ask that question.

"Did you cheat on me? Is that why you ended things before?"

Francesco looks me straight in the eye. "I *never* cheated on you, Maeve. I didn't even come close to it. I ended things because I was an immature asshole. But I promise you I never cheated."

I nod slowly. The look in his eyes is begging me to believe him. "And what about Callum? He's been there for Saoirse and me from the beginning. It's not fair to him for me to just up and leave."

"I thought you were broken up? I understand that Saoirse thinks he's her papà. And I'm guessing he will still want to be in her life. As long as you're with me, I'll find a way to deal with that."

"He asked me that same thing. He couldn't love Saoirse more even if she was his, and I can't take that away from either of them. They have a great relationship."

Francesco takes a deep breath. "Okay. I understand, and I won't fight you on that. But will you give us a second chance?"

"Yes Franco, I want to try again. But I don't know where to start. And I need to talk to Callum first."

"We're thinking of staying here for three weeks. We

can take it slow, I don't want to scare Saoirse, but I really want to meet her. And I want her to spend time with my family while they're all here. I also want us to get to know each other again."

Taking a deep breath, I nod at him. "We can try, Franco. But I can't commit to moving to Chicago with you yet. Saoirse's life is here. Her school, friends, family–they're all here. I know you're going to say she'll adapt to wherever we live, and I don't disagree. But I want her to be comfortable and I want her to feel safe."

The look on his face is not a happy one. But it's the truth. Saoirse's feelings come before any of ours. "I can't leave Ireland without both of you."

"But you can't stay here, you have a job and school, and I can't leave."

"And? You and Saoirse are more important."

"Please don't put me in that position. I know you, and you would never leave Celestino to take care of the business by himself. If we can work this out, *if* we do, then we'll discuss moving."

"Okay piccola lontra. We can do this however you feel most comfortable."

Francesco uses his pet name for me so easily. *His little otter.* He started calling me that the night we met. It was at a barbecue for the Galway chapter of the MC. We were sitting on the grass, talking, and this tiny baby otter came running up to sit with us. Eventually the mam otter came running over, making loud noises like she was scolding it. Or maybe us? Either way, she was mad and carried it away with her. But then they both came back the next day. I made sure to put some food out for them after that. Eventually, they made their home in the pond that's on the property. As far as I know, they're still there to this day. It made me sad that I couldn't go back to the clubhouse and show Saoirse the otters because of the deal I made with Cormac.

"I saw our otters when I was at the clubhouse. There's more adults now and new babies."

It's like he can hear my frickin' thoughts.

"I haven't seen them since the day I met up with Cormac. I've always wanted Saoirse to meet them."

"We'll take her there. When can I meet her?"

"She's spending the night with Callum's grandparents. So maybe tomorrow? Or the day after?"

"Tomorrow. It'll be hard enough to wait till then. I don't want to wait another day."

Now the problem is, how do you explain to your four year old that her da isn't her da? And I know Callum will want to be there when they meet. I wish my parents were here with me.

Chapter Seven

Callum

After I dropped Saoirse off with my grandparents, I decided to go have some coffee and do some thinking. Sitting here in this coffee shop, I've got the worst feeling, deep in the pit of my stomach. I'm wondering what I could've done differently. Should I have asked Maeve to marry me sooner? Maybe, but there's a part of me that knew from the start that I would never have her whole heart. I knew about Francesco and how hurt she was by what he did. Deep down, I knew she was waiting for him to come back to her and now he has.

I called my mam last night, she's the strongest woman I know. She raised me by herself until I was about ten. When my mam found out she was pregnant, my grandparents were so angry. And then she decided to keep me, which made them even angrier. But when I was ten, they came to our house and apologized for being so stubborn. I remember hearing them ask my mam for a chance to make it right. Since that day, they've been in my life. And helped raise me.

When I told my mam about my problem, she told me not to push Maeve. That this was a decision she had to make on her own. And no matter how much it hurts, I have to support her no matter what she decides. I probably should've listened to my mam. Because in my desperation this morning, I asked Maeve to marry me She didn't say no—but she didn't say yes either. She asked for time to think. And I agreed. I don't want her to marry me because I'm the safe choice. I want her to choose me because she loves me and wants to spend the rest of our lives together.

If she chooses Francesco? Well, I'll have to respect that. In the end, all I truly want is for Maeve to be happy and if that arsehole is who will make her happy? Then I'll step back and be there for her and Saoirse like I've always been. But if he hurts her again? I will make sure he suffers for it. And he'll never be able to tell me that I can't be in Maeve and Saoirse's lives.

I remember the first time I saw Maeve. She was working in the cafe I walked into on my very first night in Galway. She took my breath away, but there was sadness in her eyes. I knew then that I had to get to know her. I spent every night there having dinner just so I could spend a few hours with her. It took a few weeks before she would agree to have coffee with me. Now I know everything there is to know about Maeve. Including how that arsehole led her on and then broke her heart. And now he's back to take away the two things that mean the most to me in this world.

The hardest part about this isn't that he's back. It's that he thinks he can just tell her he's sorry and she'll immediately fall at his feet. It took a month before she told me she was pregnant. And about the baby's father. I was furious that a man would treat a woman he claimed to love the way he treated Maeve. The way he left her wasn't fair and I know that she should've told him about Saiorse, but the selfish side of me was glad she didn't. And I knew from the moment she told me her situation that I would be there for her, no matter what.

Feeling sorry for myself, I finally get up to order something to eat. I don't want to go home just yet. At that moment, a woman turns and dumps her iced coffee on me.

"Oh my god, I'm so sorry!" she exclaims.

I shiver slightly and look down at my shirt and jeans. Well, that's one way to end this crappy day. Next, I feel hands trying to dry my shirt. Those same hands brush my crotch and I hear a gasp. I look up and see the same woman blushing and throwing the rest of the napkins at me.

I'm cold and slightly sticky, but the look on her face is making me laugh.

"It's okay. Why don't you join me? You look

familiar, did I see you yesterday with the Bastianini family? You were at the Cliffs of Moher with them?"

She slowly sits down across from me and nods.

"Yes, Luciana Bastianini is one of my best friends. She got engaged yesterday. You're the guy from the cafe..."

"Aye, I am. Callum McGregor, and you are?"

"Moira Cooper."

"It's nice to meet you. Let me order you another drink. I was just about to get a bite to eat. Are you hungry?"

Even though my heart is hurting because of this situation with Maeve, when I look at Moira, something stirs in me. What the hell is wrong with me? I love Maeve. I shouldn't be looking at other women. But there's something about Moira...and it's not just her beauty.

"Please let me buy your food. It's the least I can do after dumping my coffee on you."

I chuckle. "Don't worry. I got it."

I head to the counter and tell the woman at the counter that I need a Latte and two chocolate croissants. With whip cream.

After I finish ordering, I head back to the table and sit down with Moira.

"I love your accent. Scottish?"

"Aye, born and raised in Saltcoats, it's in North Ayrshire."

"I've always wanted to visit Scotland. Where's your hometown?"

She smiles at me, and I find myself saying things I shouldn't.

"It's on the west coast of Scotland. I love it there. How long are you visiting? I could take you and show you a few places," I say as her drink and our croissants are delivered.

"We're supposed to stay for two, maybe three weeks. I would love to see Scotland with you."

The blush that spreads across her cheeks is lovely. I can't stop myself from smiling back at her. We exchange numbers. She needs to talk to her friends, and I need to check with Maeve before we can make any plans. Maybe we can make it a group trip. I would like to get to know Franco and his family before they leave.

"Well, I should get back to my friends. It was really nice meeting you, Callum. I hope we can figure out a plan to see your homeland while we are here."

I stand as she does. I reach out to take her hands in mine and give them a light squeeze.

"It was nice meeting you too, Moira. I'm sure we'll figure something out. Maybe your friends would like to see Scotland too."

She gives me a big smile. I watch her walk out of the coffee shop, and for the first time since Francesco showed up at my cafe, I feel lighter. Like maybe there's something out there for me, even if it's not with Maeve. Because right now, the only thing I'm sure of is that I need to be in Saoirse's life no matter what path our lives take.

I look at the time; I need to get off my ass and head

back home to see how Maeve's visit with Francesco went. Wish me luck.

Maeve

Francesco wanted me to stay and have dinner with the family, but I told him I needed to go home and talk to Callum. He made me promise to text him after we talked.

Sitting at home waiting for Callum to get back is torture. I still don't know how I'm going to tell him that I want to try again with Franco. I don't want him to think that I expect him to wait for me. And if I decide to move to Chicago with Saoirse...how will he see her? All these thoughts are making me crazy. Callum is the last person I would ever want to hurt. And Saoirse, my sweet girl, how do I explain to her about Francesco? How did my life go from being okay to this storm that's swirling around me?

An hour later, I hear the door open.

"Hen? Are you home?" Callum calls out.

"I'm in the living room."

He comes over and kisses the top of my head. "How did it go?"

I look up at him. I remember the first time I saw Callum, his smile made my heart smile. But I was hurting so much from Francesco and finding out that I was pregnant...I truly didn't appreciate it until now. He's rugged and handsome, like a young Gerard Butler. I hope he understands why I need to give it another try with Francesco.

"It went well. Francesco says he's forgiven me for not telling him about Saoirse. And he understands that you are who she knows as her da. But he wants to meet her and get to know her."

"And you and Francesco? Are you choosing to be with him again?"

I can already see the pain I'm causing him, and it's killing me.

"I'm so sorry, Callum. I do want to try again with him."

His head drops while he listens to me, and I see a tear fall.

"Is he going to have a problem with me being in your lives? Because if he does, he and I will have to sit and talk," he says as he wipes his face.

I shake my head. "He says he won't stand between you and Saoirse. He wants what's best for her."

"I feel a but coming on..."

I look down at my hands as I try to figure out how to tell him that Francesco wants us to move to Chicago with him.

"He wants you to go home with him, doesn't he? Back to Chicago?" His voice breaks, and a few more tears fall.

I nod slowly, trying my best to hold back my own

tears. "He asked. But I told him that I don't know if I can do that. I need to make the best decisions for Saoirse and I'm not sure if moving to Chicago right now is the right thing to do."

He looks a little relieved when I explain.

"But eventually you'll move to Chicago to be with him, right?"

"Yes. If it works out, that's what I would like to do. He can't move here, he has a business and his family obligations keep him in Chicago."

"If you move to America with Saoirse, I will, too. I can't be here in Ireland while she's in Chicago."

This man is something else. He's willing to give up the life he's created here just to be close to Saoirse.

"Thank you for being the best da to her. She's a lucky girl to have you in her life."

"Hen, I'm the lucky one. I got to spend four wonderful years with you and Saoirse. I can't say your decision to be with Francesco doesn't hurt. Because it feels like my heart is being ripped out of my chest right now. But all I've ever wanted was for you to be happy, and for Saoirse to grow up loved and protected. And if he is the one to give that to you...well then I will step back and accept it as best I can. But know that I love you both more than I can ever explain."

My tears are flowing as I listen to Callum. I can feel his pain and I hate that I'm the one causing it.

"I'm sorry. I've never wanted to hurt you. Ever. I just—I have to follow what my heart is saying. But it doesn't mean that I don't love you. Because I do."

"I know, Maeve. But I also know that you've always been waiting for Francesco to come back to you. I had hoped that he never would because then I could keep you both forever."

He pulls me closer to him and wraps his arms around me. "You'll always have a piece of my heart," he whispers.

That one sentence kills me, and I start bawling. Ugly, hiccuping bawling.

"Shh, hen. Please don't cry, we're going to be okay. Everything will work out the way it's supposed to. But I can't promise I won't beat the hell out of Francesco if he dares to hurt either of you."

That gets a small chuckle out of me. "Thank you, Callum. I want you in my life, but I don't want you to stay if it hurts you. I want you to be happy."

"I'll stay because it's what I want. Maybe one day I'll find what you have with Francesco. I wish it was with you. But know that I'm happy if you're happy, hen."

Any woman that Callum chooses to love will be one lucky lady. She better treat him right. I hope Callum stays in mine and Saoirse's lives forever.

Chapter Eight

Francesco

The first thing I think of this morning is Saoirse. I can't wait to meet my daughter. Last night, Maeve told me she goes to Junior Infants. It's the equivalent to preschool in Chicago.. Since we don't want to disrupt her schedule too much, the plan is for me to meet them at the beach this afternoon. Well, not just me, my whole family. My parents are so excited to meet their first grandchild. Saoirse doesn't know it yet, but she's about to be the most loved little girl ever. And Maeve is going to get back the family she always wanted. I can't wait.

"How are you doing, Son?" my mam asks as she joins me in the kitchen.

"I'm nervous. What if Saoirse doesn't want to be

with me? Callum has been her papà, he's all she knows, I'm just a stranger."

My mam comes over and hugs me. She gives the best hugs.

"It's going to take time, baby. You're right, she doesn't know you. But she will get to know you, get to know all of us. And you need to hold to what you told Maeve. That you'll support Callum being in Saoirse's life."

I frown at my mam.

"I know what I said. But I don't know if I can do that."

"You're going to have to. You don't get to tell Maeve something like that and then go back on your word. We didn't raise you to be that kind of person. We raised you to be honest and truthful. And besides, you can't do that to your daughter. I won't let you."

Fuck. The look of disapproval on my mam's face is killing me. And she's right. No matter how much it fucking hurts, I need to do my best to get along with Callum. From what I know of him, he's a good person. I mean, he *has* taken care of my girls.

"Okay, Mam. I will do everything I can to support Maeve and Saoirse. Even if that means accepting Callum will be around too."

She smiles and wraps her arms around me. "That's the son I raised. Things will work out the way they're supposed to. It'll take time, but it will be okay."

I really hope my mam is right. I'm not letting

Maeve go again. I was dumb before and I won't make the same mistake again.

"We were all planning on going with you to meet Saoirse. I know it might be a lot for her, but if she seems like it's getting to be too much, we'll leave."

"That sounds good. I'm still so nervous. Who would've thought that a four-year-old girl could be so scary?" I chuckle.

My mam laughs. "Just wait. She's going to have you wrapped around her finger in no time."

"I think she already does and I haven't even met her."

"Who does what?" My papà asks as he joins us.

"I told Franco that Saoirse is going to have him wrapped around her finger in no time." My mam says.

My papà laughs and wraps his arms around her. "She's going to have all of us bowing down to her."

The look on both my parents' faces is pure joy. They were so happy when I told them about Saoirse. Not once did they ask if I was sure she was mine.

We all gather outside to head to the ferry. While we're in Ireland, we're staying on Inishmore, the largest of the Aran Islands. It's where Rónán and his brothers are from. We were planning to stay with our grandparents, but Rónán asked if we would stay on the island because he wanted to show us where he grew up. His parents own one of the three restaurants on the island. It's beautiful here and I can't wait to show Maeve and Saoirse. I'm not sure if Maeve has been to the islands, but I'm hoping there are some areas of Ireland that we can experience for the first time together.

While we wait for the ferry, I look at my family. Now that Luciana is engaged, our family is growing. Maeve always talked about how she wished she had siblings, or even cousins. Her parents didn't have siblings, and she's an only child too. My family is her family even if she chooses not to be with me...Fuck that. She's mine. I'll win her back.

I've never been this nervous. And all because I'm meeting a four-year-old little girl. A little girl that I already love more than life itself.

"I'm thinking of staying for three weeks," I say to my papà.

"I figured you would. Your mam and I already talked and we'll head home in two weeks, as planned. But everyone else will stay here with you."

"They don't have to stay. You need them back at home for club stuff."

"I think the club can survive an extra week without some of its officers." He laughs. "Saoirse and Maeve are important, not just to you, but to our family."

I smile at my papà. "Thanks, Papà. I'm just so thankful Maeve is giving me another chance."

"You remember that feeling when times get hard. Because no matter what, times will get rough. But it's how you choose to deal with it that matters most."

Maeve

"Where are we going, Mam? Where's Da?"

My girl doesn't miss anything. I still haven't figured out how to tell her about Franco. And now I have about an hour to explain it to my baby.

"Da is busy at the cafe. This is an outing for just the two of us," I say. It seems to satisfy her for the moment.

"Can we get ice cream? I was really good in school today."

I chuckle. The way that Saoirse says she was good in school today makes it sound like she's normally not good. And I love the way she's trying to pronounce words, she's getting so much better.

"Sure, love. We can get some ice cream a little later, okay?"

"Okay, Mam." She smiles at me in the mirror and then starts singing the alphabet.

I find a parking spot and take a few deep breaths. Maybe a walk will be good for us—we can find a spot to stop and I can try to explain to her what's happening.

"You ready?" I smile at her as I get her out of her seat.

"I love the beach!" She giggles.

"Why don't we stop here and sit. Mam needs to tell you something."

"Okay, Mam. Am I in trouble?"

"No, baby. You're not in trouble. I need you to listen for a bit."

She's staring at me and nodding. "Okay, Mam."

"You're going to meet some people today. They're good people and they're your family."

"You and Da are my family. And Granda and Granny and Nana."

"We are, baby. But you have a lot more family than just us."

She's frowning at me now.

"But I don't know them? Why?"

"That's a hard question to answer, baby. One day I'll explain all of it. Right now, all you need to know is that everyone here loves you and wants the best for you."

Okay, part one done. Now how the fuck do I explain that Callum isn't her da? Saoirse reaches out and hugs me. I take several deep breaths, I can't start crying in front of her. Maybe we can ease into this when Franco gets here. She's only four years old. I don't even know how much she will really understand. I explained to Franco that I don't know how to tell her. He said he understood, and we'll find a way to do it together.

Francesco

The ride from the ferry to Salt Hill beach seems to take forever. As we're all spilling out of the car, I spot Maeve and Saoirse waiting for us. My heart is beating so damn fast. My girls.

It takes everything in me not to run over and scoop them up in my arms. I'm not sure what Maeve has told Saoirse about me yet. When we talked, she wanted to take it slow. I get it. I don't like it, but I get it. I don't want to scare my daughter either.

I'm finally standing in front of my daughter and I kneel to her level.

"Hi," I whisper as I memorize every detail of her face.

"You have the same color eyes as me," she says in her beautiful Irish accent. She's staring at me like she's memorizing me too.

"I do. But I think yours are prettier than mine."

She giggles and looks up at everyone who's surrounding us.

Maeve

Watching Saoirse's first meeting with Franco brings tears to my eyes. She focuses on the one thing that's always reminded me of Franco. Her eyes. They're his eyes, not just the color, it's the shape. And they both have long curly eyelashes. The rest of her features are mine. But those eyes and dimples...that's all Franco.

"She's beautiful, Maeve," Franco's mam, Caitríona, whispers to me.

"Thank you. She's my life."

"I know you're afraid that Franco will leave again and try to take her from you. He'll never do that. You have my word," she says, looking at me.

I had forgotten how much I loved Franco's parents. They never treated me like I was less than their own children. Fairness was something I always got from them, they never took their kids' side just because. If the kids were wrong, they were told they were wrong.

"Thank you, Caitríona," I say, holding back my tears.

"I was 'Mam' before. I can be that again if you want." She hugs me. "I'm very sorry you lost your nana."

Mam. I haven't had a mam for so long.

"Mam," I whisper. "Thank you."

"Don't forget me. Papàs are just as important," I hear Giacomo say as he wraps his arms around both of us.

This family meant so much to me before. Can they really be willing to embrace me again? I know they love Saoirse, but she's their blood. I'm not.

"You're our family too. Not just Saoirse," Caitríona says.

Did I say that out loud? The look on her face says no, so how does she do that?

"Mam has that sixth sense, she just knows what you're thinking." Luciana laughs.

"Made it really hard to get away with things while we were growing up," Celestino adds.

Everyone starts laughing. This is the family I remember, watching them laugh and joke with each other. And now there's more of them with the addition of Luciana and Isabella's friends. There are four girls and one guy, plus the O'Callaghan brothers. I always wanted a big family, and when I was with Franco before, I had it. It was really hard when I lost them. Now they're back like they never left. And the family has multiplied like tribbles, they're adorable. From what I can see, they're just like the Bastianini family. Loyal and protective.

Saoirse can't stop smiling at all of them. And then she asks the one thing I've been dreading.

"Mam said you're family. My family?"

Everyone turns and looks at me. Fuck.

"Saoirse? Remember, Mam said she'll explain it later. But yes, they're all your family," I say.

"I forgot." She giggles.

"It's okay, I forget lots of things." Franco laughs.

"You forget too?" She looks at him with her big eyes.

"Yep. What's your name again?" he teases.

Saoirse laughs more. "Silly. My name is Saoirse

Liliana Bastianini, and I'm four." She holds up four fingers.

As soon as my baby blurts out her name, everyone stops talking. I think I hear someone gasp. Franco stands and turns to face me.

"Bastianini?" he whispers.

Dammit.

"Yes. I wanted her to know who she is," I say softly.

"Why you whispering, Mam? You said no whispering if there's people around. It's rude."

"I'm sorry, love. That's my fault. We won't whisper anymore," Franco says, saving me from Saoirse's wrath.

Instead, she squints up at him, making a noise and frowning at him. She may be four, but I've always felt like she has an old soul.

Francesco's family starts to introduce themselves to her and I can see the joy on her face as she realizes how many of them there are.

"Why don't we head to the clubhouse? We can show Saoirse the otters," Francesco says to me as we watch her get to know his family.

"That would be fun. I miss those otters. And you said there's more of them now? Did they remember you?"

"They did, piccola lontra. The Mam and Da otters came up to me after a few minutes. They seemed a little timid at first, but then they warmed back up."

"I can't wait to see them again, and I know Saoirse is going to love them."

"There were quite a few more, now. Cormac said

that the whole club makes sure they're all taken care of."

"I love that they kept taking care of them. I worried that they would stop."

I feel a tug on the bottom of my shirt. I see Saoirse looking up at me.

"Why do you call my mam piccola lontra, what is that?" She asks me.

I smile and crouch down to her level.

"I call your mam piccola lontra because she reminds me of the little otters that live at the clubhouse. Piccola means little and lontra is an otter." I explain to her.

"What's a clubhouse? And why do they live there?"

"The clubhouse is where my friends live and the otters live there with them."

"Can we go and see them?"

"Yes. We will go and see them soon."

Saoirse gives Franco a hug. We watch her run over to Franco's parents and they embrace her. My life with Callum was always fulfilling. But this—this is what I always dreamed of.

"Maeve, thank you for today. I never dreamed that I would have a second chance to make things right with you. You have always been my life and I promise I won't make the same mistakes twice."

Franco leans down and captures my lips with his. This is home, the feelings swirling around in my heart and head as we share our first kiss back together—this is what forever feels like.

"What do you think about taking a trip to Scotland?" I ask Franco.

"Sure, that would be fun. Do you mean everyone?" He asks.

"Yes. Callum grew up in Scotland and he wants to show everyone his island. And he wants you to meet him mam, Fiona. Plus this way Saoirse can spend some time with her too."

Franco nods at me. "That sounds nice. My mam was just saying how she hoped she would be able to meet Callum's mam. We all want to thank her for taking care of you and Saoirse."

I hug Franco. "She's going to love you."

Chapter Nine

Maeve

Today we're headed to Scotland, where Callum grew up. It's a gorgeous seaside town called Saltcoats, on the west coast of North Ayrshire. We go there several times a year, because his mam, Fiona, still lives there in the house she raised him in. She comes to visit us a lot too. The trip from her home to us is an eight-hour drive or one hour on a plane—after a two-and-a-half hour drive to Dublin. His grandparents live here in Ireland. Their original plan was to just be here for a little while to help us with Saoirse when she was a baby, but they love being with her so much they stayed. His mam wanted to join us here, but she owns a small gift shop in their town. She didn't want to sell it or hire someone to run it for her.

"Are you okay with this trip?" I ask Francesco.

"Yeah, I'm good. I love Scotland, and I really want to get to know Callum better."

I hug him tight. "Thank you. You're going to love Callum's mam. She's a great person, and she loves Saoirse so much."

"It makes me happy that you and Saoirse had such a great support system. I still wish I hadn't left you when I did. It should've been me and my family taking care of you." He says sadly.

"We both made our mistakes and now we're fixing them. I got lucky meeting Callum and having his mam and grandparents around. But they didn't take your place, they just helped me get through not having you with us."

He smiles and kisses me. I love the feeling of his lips on mine. Every time he kisses me, I get that fluttery feeling in my tummy. I hope it never stops.

After arriving at Glasgow International, we take the train to Saltcoats. We rented a car when we arrived at the airport. Callum's mam offered to come and get us, but there's twenty-three of us plus Saoirse. We'd never fit in her tiny car—we barely fit when it's just Callum, me, Saoirse, her car seat and our luggage. We're staying at a bed and breakfast that's about fifteen minutes from his mam's house. We rented the whole house. Our other option was to stay at a hotel, but that would mean a lot of rooms and they could be scattered all around the hotel. This way, we are all together in one place.

We'll be staying here for four days. Callum is so excited to show everyone his hometown. I've also noticed that he and Moira have been smiling and whispering to each other. It makes my heart happy if he's found someone to be with. And if it's one of Luciana's friends? Even better.

We drop our things off at the Bed and Breakfast then head to Fiona's house. Her home was originally a small two-bedroom cottage. After Callum graduated from University and bought the cafe at the Cliffs, he did some renovations. Now it has four bedrooms and four bathrooms. He's also redone her kitchen and fenced in her property. That was the one thing he wanted to do for his mam. She raised him all by herself and he said he never once heard her complain, even though he knew she struggled.

"NANA!" Saoirse yells while running into Fiona's arms.

"My sweet girl!" Fiona laughs as she swings her around.

"I have more family now, Nana! Come see!"

Saoirse excitedly pulls Fiona to the group and starts introducing her to everyone.

"I won't remember all your names right away, but I will, in time." She laughs. "It's so nice to meet all of you. Are you hungry? We can have lunch at one of the restaurants that's within walking distance, then we can tour the town."

"You have a beautiful home," Caitríona says to Fiona.

"Thank you. This is all because of my Callum. It used to be a small cottage, just two small bedrooms, one bathroom living room and kitchen. Two years ago, he sent me to Italy for a month and when I came back, he had done all the renovations as a gift." You can see the pride and love shining in her eyes as she looks at Callum.

"It's the least I could do for you, Mam. You gave me everything you could while I was growing up."

She chuckles. "You're my son, of course I gave you everything I could."

This is why Callum is such a good person. His mam is the best, she sacrificed so much for him. He said he always knew he wanted to give back to her. Then came the day he could finally afford to give back to her. He booked her a trip to Italy for a month. It took that whole month to finish the renovations; I was lucky enough to be there when she came home to it. It was a spectacular day.

Francesco wraps his arms around me from behind, and I lean back into him. We take a minute to watch everyone around us. It makes my heart so happy to see everyone getting along.

"She seems like a really great woman and a great addition to our family. I can tell my parents and grandparents already like her," he whispers in my ear.

My smile gets even bigger hearing him say that. I was worried that there might be some animosity between the families. But watching Francesco's family talking with Fiona, my fears are dissolving. I know we can make this work, for Saoirse. The happiness on her face is amazing to see. She's flitting back and forth between everyone.

Callum's grandparents are arriving later today. It makes me so happy to know that both families will have the chance to get to know each other.

Francesco

Meeting Callum's mam went a lot better than I was expecting. I didn't know what to be prepared for. Was she going to hate me right away because of what I did to Maeve and Saoirse?

She embraced me the same way she embraced her son and everyone else in our group. Her smile was genuine, and I felt no anger coming from her. It was amazing. She's already exchanged numbers with my parents and I have a feeling we're going to be seeing her a lot.

Scotland is just as beautiful as Ireland. The coastal village that Callum grew up in reminds me of Galway. I love that Saoirse has been able to spend a lot of time here. Sitting on the beach, I'm so grateful that Maeve has given me a second chance. Now my only worry is about how she's going to deal with my job. It's one thing for her to know about it and another actually seeing it. The women that come to our shows can get pretty aggressive. There are times my sisters have had to hold back their anger at the shows. Especially when the women act inappropriately towards their men.

A voice breaks into my thoughts. "Please promise me that you'll take care of Maeve and Saoirse," Fiona says, sitting down next to me.

I turn to look at her. "I will. I know I made a mistake before, but I won't be doing that again. Thank you for loving them all these years."

"They're my family. Just because you're back with Maeve doesn't mean you can take Saoirse away from me and from my son."

There's fear in her voice, yet she has the strength to say this to me. She's not really asking me. She's telling me.

"I would never deny you or Callum access to Saoirse. Neither would any of my family. When we were growing up, our parents taught that family is the core of our lives. Even our club life. You, your parents and Callum are now part of our family."

I see her thinking about this. "Thank you, Francesco. Maeve always said you were a good person who made a bad decision. I'm glad to see she was right. I won't pretend that I wish you hadn't come back, because I know that it's hurting my son. But I am happy that you are the man Maeve said you were."

Blinking back tears, I reach out and hug her. Even after hurting her only son, she's found a way to accept me. She hugs me back tightly.

"Your parents raised a good man," she says softly.

"Thank you. I've made my mistakes, but I learned from them. And I won't be repeating them. Maeve has always had my heart. There's been no one who's ever come close to how she makes me feel."

"I see the way you look at Maeve and that shows me how much you love her. I know you won't make the same mistakes. And thank you for embracing my family." She smiles at me. "Come on, let me show my new family my home."

The four days we spent in Scotland went by faster than I thought it would. I love the town that Callum grew up in. It's the complete opposite of Chicago, where I grew up. Fiona invited us to come visit anytime we want and I think we'll be coming back as often as we can.

Today we're taking Saoirse to the Cimaruta clubhouse. I want to introduce her to my Irish brothers and the otters. We haven't told her she's going to meet anyone, I want it to be a surprise.

"I'm so excited to see the otter family again," Maeve says as she gets ready. "I can't wait to see the new adults and babies."

"I saw four new adults and several babies. They even have a veterinarian that comes out once a month to look at all the otters."

"That's so wonderful, I'm so glad the guys kept taking care of them." She smiles. "Let's get going. I can't wait any longer."

"We should have a picnic. Or we can have one of the prospects make us lunch." He chuckles.

"We can make sandwiches before we go. That way, we don't have to bother the guys in the clubhouse. I'm not sure I want Saoirse seeing the bunnies."

"You know she's going to have to see what club life is like eventually. But I can give Cormac a heads up so the bunnies behave."

Maeve sighs at me. "I know she will, but do you ever really know if they'll be dressed when you walk in there? Do you think Cormac will mind if the bunnies aren't around just for today?"

I think about what she's saying. "You're right, piccola lontra. We're changing that the next time we have church.

Papà wants it to be more family friendly and with Mam and my sisters on the council, it's more respectful for the bunnies to be clothed. And no, I don't think he will mind."

"That would be nice, I wish all the clubs would do that. That's always been one thing that made me uncomfortable, even when I was younger and would go to the club with my da," she says as she makes our lunch.

I get some drinks and a few small bags of chips, and add them to the basket Maeve has produced for our picnic. Then I give Cormac a call.

Maeve

I never thought I'd be back at the MC clubhouse. I'm glad I didn't visit the otters before, because the minute I see them, all the memories of being with Franco come flooding back. The day we met the original baby and her mam. They're still here, and it's like no time has passed.

"Are you ready for your surprise?" Franco asks Saoirse.

"Yes! I love surprises!" She giggles.

"You have to be careful and don't yell or run when you meet the surprise. Okay?"

She looks at him with her serious face.

"Okay. I'll be good," she whispers back at him.

"Do you see those otters there by the pond?" he asks.

"Yes. They live here?"

"They do live here. See the one with the red collar? That's the first one that came to live here with her baby," he explains to her.

"They are so little," she says, still whispering.

"Would you like to get closer? As long as you're nice and don't yell or run at them, they'll love you."

She nods at him and takes his hand. Watching them is making my heart so happy, I never imagined it would be like this when they met. I mean, I hoped, but I never really let myself believe it. It hurt too much. I go over to them and the three of us walk down to the edge of the pond. I lay out the blanket we brought and sit down to start taking out the goodies we brought for us and the otters.

"Can I feed them?" Saoirse asks.

"Of course you can," I say, handing her a few grapes.

"Later on, we can hide some of the treats around the pond," Franco says. "And watch them look for them."

"Hide them? That's mean." Saoirse scrunches up her little face at him.

He laughs and kisses her nose.

"It's not mean, the otters like searching for food. It makes them happy," he says.

"But isn't it nice to give it to them?"

"It is nice, but they enjoy looking around too. We can sit and watch them after we hide some."

"Hmm. Okay," she says, not sounding like she believes him at all. It makes me laugh. Looking at the two of them, I realize just how much she looks like Franco. I always saw it in her eyes, but now I see so many other features and facial expressions that are Franco's.

After our weekend in Scotland, I've been thinking more and more about moving to Chicago. On one hand, I'm so damn scared he'll change his mind again. And on the other, I want to let that fear go.

"Can we hide their snacks now, *Da Lontra?*" Saoirse asks Franco.

I chuckle at her calling him 'Da Lontra.'

"Yes, amore, we can hide their snacks. You want to help us, piccola lontra?"

I nod and get up, grabbing the snacks we brought for them.

"Hide all these?" she asks.

"We can hide as many as you want. Then we can eat our lunch while we wait for them to find their treats," Franco answers.

Saoirse giggles and nods. "Okay, Da Lontra."

Chapter Ten

Maeve

I snuggle into Franco as I start to wake up. These last three weeks have flown by too fast. I'm not ready to say goodbye to him, and he leaves in two days. Saoirse has become so attached to him and his family. He keeps asking me to move to Chicago...but I don't know if I can do that yet. Being with Saoirse and me while on vacation differs from regular everyday life. I'm afraid that he'll realize it's too much. Then I'm left with a four year old that won't understand why her da doesn't want her. Oh, and a broken heart that I don't think will heal a second time.

"Morning, amore." His raspy morning voice is so damn sexy.

I'm lying next to him, breathing him in and my head floods with memories I have treasured for years.

Francesco murmurs his apologies. Every morning while he holds me close, he apologizes for leaving me. This time as he's apologizing to me, he starts kissing my face. He continues his apologies by kissing my neck, slipping my tank top off. He continues kissing down my chest pausing over each breast, taking his tongue and licking each of my nipples, teasing them until they show the arousal he is looking for. Then takes my breasts in his hands and pinches my nipples. That sends jolts throughout my body. He continues kissing down my stomach, still caressing my breasts. I run my fingers through his hair.

"Baby, this is for you, I want to show you how much I missed you, how sorry I am for everything I did. I want to love you like you deserve to loved."

Francesco pulls my shorts down, kissing my hips. He makes his way down and slowly licks circles over my clit, then thrusts his tongue into my pussy. It sends ripples of pleasure roaring through my body. He slides his finger around my slit, finally pushing one into me, which pushes me over the edge. As I climax, he is still licking me and murmuring how much he missed the taste of me. When I finally come back down, I push him onto his back and run my hand down his stomach, memorizing every inch of his body. Then slowly continue my way down and trace a line from the tip of his cock to his balls. His moan is the sexiest sound I've ever heard. I slide my way down his body, exchanging my tongue for my hand eliciting a rumbling noise out of him. I slowly lick him, following the same path I made with my hand.

"Maeve..." he moans.

Before I can finish licking my way back up, he's flipping me on my back and he's inside me. He stops to give me a minute to adjust to him. But all I want him to do is fuck me.

"Oh fuck, Franco," I gasp, grabbing his ass.

"Fuck, I missed being inside you."

He's teasing me now, moving in and out as slow as he can.

"Stop fucking teasing me," I growl.

"Tell me what you want, baby."

"Fuck me. I want you to fuck me."

He smiles at me and captures my mouth with his. I nip his lip, knowing this will make him crazy.

"Oh god yes. Franco. Fuck. Baby," I babble incoherently as he moves in and out of me faster.

"Fuck, Maeve. I love you. Come for me, baby."

Hearing him say he loves me always sends me over the edge. This orgasm is stronger, and it sends him pulsing in me at the same time. He holds me tight while we both catch our breath.

"I love you too, Franco," I say softly, looking into his beautiful blue-green eyes.

I haven't said that to him until now. That fear I have kept me from saying it. But I've felt it. In fact, I've never *not* loved him, even when he left me.

His arms wrap tighter around me. "You're it for me,

Maeve. I know you're still having a hard time believing me. But it's okay, because soon you'll see that I'm never letting you go."

I want to believe him, and the look in his eyes pleads with me to believe him.

Francesco

Maeve finally said she loves me. I've been saying it since the day I saw her again. I'm not ready to leave my girls, three weeks is nowhere near enough time to get to know my daughter and show Maeve that my intentions are real. That this isn't a game that I'm playing. But I don't know how to do it.

I don't know how to convince Maeve that moving to Chicago with me is the right thing to do. But I know in my heart that we will be a family soon.

Saoirse is the sweetest little girl. Maeve and Callum have done such a great job raising her. Now it's time for me to step up and be her papà. I'm hoping one day soon she'll call me 'Papà'. Right now she calls me 'da lontra.' That started the day I met her and we took her to see the family of otters that live on the Cimaruta property. The look on her face as she watched the little animals was pure joy. Ever since Saoirse heard me call Maeve 'piccola lontra', she's been calling me da lontra, I'm guessing because of what I call her mam.

"I love you Maeve. I've loved you since the day I

saw you at the clubhouse when we were fourteen years old. Even back then I knew you were the one for me."

"I knew then too, Franco. That's why I was so confused when you left me. I thought we were moving forward. I was planning on moving to Chicago to go to school and be with you."

"I was a coward, and I was stupid. But there wasn't a day went by that I didn't think of you."

"Were you scared of making a permanent commitment? Was it the women?"

I can hear the uncertainty in her voice. It's not like my job has changed since then, if anything it's gotten busier with the club and shows.

"It wasn't the women, not in the way you're thinking. I didn't want them, but they were throwing themselves at us and I didn't know how to handle it back then. But I swear to you I never touched any of them when we were together. I *never* cheated on you."

"And after? I know it wasn't cheating after we broke up...but did you sleep with the women that came to your shows? Or the private shows that you do?"

I don't want to lie to Maeve, but I don't want her to feel insecure about our relationship either. So I don't know how to answer that question. Fuck.

"Once in a while. It wasn't something I did normally. I couldn't give my time or love to anyone because I've always belonged to you. My heart was never free to give to anyone."

"Are you telling me this just to try and make me feel better?"

"I'm telling you the truth, amore. I realized that being with those women didn't do anything for me. They weren't you. I just didn't know how to get back to you. When Luciana said we were coming to Ireland, I wanted to find a way to see you. But I honestly didn't know where to start. When I saw you at the cafe, it was like fate was giving me another chance."

"Why didn't you call? Or come back to Ireland before that?" she asks.

"I didn't think you'd want to see me again. We were supposed to come to Ireland once, about two years ago. But we had too many shows booked and we couldn't leave. Mam and papà came back and stayed for a few days. I asked if they saw you but they said they hadn't."

I wipe the tears that are falling down her face.

"You'll never know how sorry I am that I didn't call or come back. After those first couple of years, it got harder and harder until it seemed impossible. All I kept thinking was what if you rejected me? Even though I knew I would've deserved it, I just couldn't do it."

"I understand," she says. "I had the same fear, that's what kept me from calling you."

"We can make this work, but we have to make a promise. I know we're getting to know each other again, but we can't hold things back from each other. It's not going to be easy, but I know we can do it."

"I agree, and no lying either. We need to be able to tell each other everything. Even if we know the other won't like it."

I wrap my arms around her. "We're gonna make it

through this. And hopefully soon you and Saoirse will come and join me in Chicago."

Maeve

We haven't told Saoirse that Franco is leaving in a few days. I'm hoping she'll understand why we can't go with him right now. I can't uproot both our lives just yet.

"I hear little feet coming towards this way." Franco chuckles as he pulls on a pair of shorts. "I'm going to miss our mornings."

I hate the sadness in his voice because I know I can take it all away by just saying we'll move to Chicago. One day I'll be able to.

"I'm going to miss this too. And I'm going to miss you. A lot."

"Then come to Chicago," he says softly. "We'll keep being a family."

"Just because we're here and you're there doesn't mean we're not a family."

"I know, I didn't mean it like that. I just meant that we can all be together, we don't have to be apart."

"I'm not ready, Franco. That doesn't mean I don't love you or that I don't want to be with you. I'm just not ready to make that big of a change yet. It's not never, it's not yet."

"I love you and I love our daughter. But I understand. I'm sorry I keep pushing you to move."

"I know why you want us to come to Chicago, I'm going to miss you too. It's something I know in time we will do, I just can't do it now."

He pushes me back on the bed and kisses me. We hear a knock and the door open.

"Kissing again?" We hear a giggly voice say.

Franco jumps off the bed and scoops Saoirse up in his arms. She squeals with laughter as she wraps her arms around his neck. He brings her over to our bed and we spend a few minutes snuggling together. It's one of my new favorite things to do in the morning.

"Are you going to stay here forever?" Saoirse asks Franco.

"Such a serious face, amore." He kisses her nose.

"Are you?" She frowns at him.

"I wish I could. But I have to get back to Chicago. I have work and school."

Saoirse sits up and gives him her best *'I don't like it'* look.

"But we're family. Families stay together. You're my da lontra."

Franco takes a deep breath, trying to keep his emotions at bay.

"I don't want to leave you. I have to go, but I promise you this. We will be back together soon."

"You can't break promises. Mam says that's bad."

"It is bad to break promises. I won't break my promise."

She launches herself into his arms as she sniffles. "I love you. I don't want you to leave."

I watch him hold her tight, as a few rogue tears escape his eyes and fall into her hair.

"I will always be here for you. You can call or text me anytime you want. You are my heart," he whispers to her.

My heart is breaking for my two loves. Maybe I'm being selfish by not moving with Franco now? I don't want my baby girl to hurt because of me. I wish I knew the right thing to do.

Franco wraps his arms around both of us.

"Squishing the baby." Saoirse giggles.

We both laugh and squish her more. I'm definitely going to miss this.

Chapter Eleven

Maeve

"When are you planning on leaving?" Callum asks.

"I'm not sure yet. I was thinking next month, I really don't want to wait much longer, Franco's been gone for three weeks. And Saoirse...well, she misses him too."

"I know, hen. I'm glad that things with Franco are going well, it makes me feel better about you and Saoirse moving there to be with him. We've had a few talks and I don't think he's going to fuck up again."

"You mean you and Franco talked about us?"

"Aye, I had to make sure for myself that he was sincere. I couldn't let him hurt you again."

When Franco left with his family, I still didn't know when I would join him in Chicago. It's such a huge decision to make especially after what we've already gone through. And this time it's not just me I have to worry about.

After he left, I realized how much I missed him. Even Saoirse has commented that she misses Franco. She's never said it in front of Callum, it's like she knows it would hurt his feelings. And she won't call Franco da, not yet anyway. Right now she keeps calling him 'da lontra.' Daddy Otter. I'm not sure why she calls him that, maybe because she heard him call me 'piccola lontra.'

Franco and Saoirse got to spend three weeks together. I'm still amazed that Saoirse just accepted what we told her.

Callum and Franco seem to have come to some sort of truce. And now I know why. I had no idea Callum had talked to Franco about me. But in the end, they both know they have to get along, for Saoirse's sake.

"I need a few months to get the cafe in order and then I'll join you in Chicago. I've started interviewing people for manager positions."

"You know you don't have to move to Chicago to stay in Saoirse's life, right?"

He smiles at me. "I know, hen. But I want to, I want to be there for both of you."

Callum looks a little nervous.

"There's also something I wanted to tell you."

I look at him and wait for him to continue.

"I think I met someone." He laughs "I mean I met

someone, but I don't know if she feels the same about me."

I can see the flush in his cheeks as he reveals this information to me.

"Is she someone I know?"

"Aye. She's a friend of Luciana."

So I wasn't going crazy when we took the trip to Scotland with everyone. I thought I saw Callum watching Moira a little more than the others.

"It's Moira, isn't it?"

The smile on Callum's face is so bright. I'm truly happy for him, and I hope she feels the same way he does. Am I jealous? Not even a little. I love that he's found someone to make him light up like that. And the fact that it's someone from Luciana's group of friends? That makes it even more special. Because this means that they'll both be in our lives. Everyone wins.

"Aye, Moira. We met at the coffee shop the day you went to talk to Francesco."

"I thought I noticed you two spending more time together on our trip to Scotland. I'm so happy for you, Callum. Is she the reason you want to come to Chicago with us?"

"Saoirse is my number one reason, Maeve. Please don't think that I'll forget her or you. But aye, Moira is the other part of my reason for wanting to go now. It wasn't before when I told you I would go with you."

"All I can say is she better treat you well. You deserve to be with someone who gives you their whole heart. I'm sorry I couldn't give you all of mine."

Callum comes over and hugs me. "I knew from the start what you were offering me. I won't lie and say I wish you had let Francesco go completely. But I understand you Maeve. I told you before that you'll always hold a piece of my heart and I meant it. You were the first one to show me what it means to really be in love, to have a family. To love someone else so much that it's like watching your heart walking around outside your body. So no matter what happens, you and Saoirse will always be my family."

I'm relieved when Callum says that. There's never going to be a time when I don't need or want him in my life and Saoirse's. He's done so much for us from the start and he never demanded anything from me in return. We will never be romantic with each other again, but he will always be one of my best friends. Saoirse is a lucky girl, she has so many people in her life now that love her and would do anything for her.

I hug him back. "You'll always be part of my family too, Callum. Thank you for these last four years. I don't know if I would be where I am now if I didn't have you."

"You're stronger than you give yourself credit for, hen. You would've made Saoirse's life the best you could. I have no doubt about that."

I shrug my shoulders, I don't have the confidence in myself that he does. I don't know where Saoirse and I would be without him.

"I wish I felt that way. I don't know what I would've done if I was alone. I was so scared when I met you. The thought of being a single mam was terrifying."

"After getting to know Francesco, I do believe he would've done the right thing if you had told him. I know why you didn't, but know that I believe him. He knew he lost the best thing in his life when he walked away from you."

Even after all the hurt I've caused him, he's still in my corner supporting me. I burst into tears as I hug him.

"Shhh. It's okay, hen. You've never been alone and you'll never be alone."

"I'm so sorry that I hurt you, Callum. You deserve so much more, and I hope Moira is the one to give it to you."

"I would do it all the same no matter the outcome, Maeve. Don't ever doubt that."

Francesco

I've been home for three weeks now and it's driving me insane that I had to leave Maeve and Saoirse back in Ireland. And to top it off? She still hasn't decided if she'll move here to Chicago. The beast in me wants to fly back to Ireland, pack them up and bring them home with me. Tie them up if I have to. But the logical, sane side of me knows better.

I've been trying to keep busy. School is back in session so there's that and of course the club. I make sure to text Maeve throughout the day and call her before Saoirse goes to bed. If I'm at a show or private, I make sure she knows that I'll be early or late in calling. I don't want her to ever feel like she's second to anything ever again.

Hearing Saoirse call Callum 'Da' still makes me crazy. But I'm not sure she'll ever stop calling him that. Maybe when she finally calls me 'Papà', it won't make me feel so sad. I loved spending those three weeks with her. She's so smart and loving. I can't help but wish I hadn't missed all those years with them. I have a lot to make up to them both.

I've also gotten to know Callum a little better. I wish I could say he's an asshole, but I can't. He's actually a really good guy. He stepped in and took care of my girls after I fucked it all up. And even now, he's stepped back and let me take over. I don't think I could be that good of a person if I was in his shoes. From what Maeve says, he's even thinking of moving to Chicago if she does. Not because he's hoping to win her back, but because he wants to be there for Saoirse. How can you hate someone like that?

I'm not sure what he'll do for work if he moves here. I know he owns the cafe at the Cliffs of Moher. So maybe he doesn't need to work? I could offer him a spot with Magic Nights Chicago. I don't know his thoughts on stripping, but who knows–he might want to give it a shot.

Now I need to figure out how to get my girls here. I'm going crazy, and it's only been three weeks. This six hour time difference sucks, it's seven in the morning here and one in the afternoon there.

Francesco: Morning, my love. Well afternoon for you lol. How is your day going?

Maeve: Afternoon, my love. It's going well. The cafe has been pretty busy, lots of people visiting the cliffs

Francesco: I miss the cliffs and I miss you and Saoirse

Maeve: We miss you too

Francesco: Please come to Chicago. Not for a visit. For good

Maeve: Okay

I think I'm hallucinating. Did Maeve finally say okay to moving here?

Francesco: Okay??

Maeve: Yes (Cheesy smile emoji)

Holy shit! My girls are coming to live with me. I'm too excited to keep texting Maeve so I call her.

*"**Hello**,"* she answers.

"Amore. You're serious, right? You and Saoirse are coming to live with me?"

"Yes. I was thinking we need about a month to prepare, and Callum said he will join us in a few months. He needs to take care of things with the cafe."

"This is the best news ever. Even with Callum coming," I tease.

"I'm still scared, Franco. This is such a big step, but I want to be with you."

"I swear you won't regret this, Maeve. I love you and Saoirse with everything I have. I won't make the same mistake I did before."

"I'm holding you to that, Franco. Because I don't think I could go through that again. And Saoirse? I won't let anyone hurt her... even you."

"I know, Maeve. I plan on spending the rest of my life showing both of you how sorry I am."

I hear her chuckle.

"I don't think it'll take the rest of our lives. But it will take some time for me to truly let go of the fear."

"I know. I love you. I never stopped, everything I did reminded me of how stupid I was to let you go. But now you're back and I won't be taking that for granted. On top of it all, you've given me the best gift I could ever ask for."

"I love you too, Franco. More than I ever wanted to admit to myself. But I have to go, there are customers coming in. Talk tonight?"

"Of course. I'll be calling at about seven your time. I love you."

"Okay, talk to you then. I love you."

She's coming. She's finally made the decision to come here and really give us a chance. I'm a little worried about how Maeve will handle the club and the women that come to our shows. My sisters have said that they'll help her in any way they can. Luciana had her issues with Rónán stripping but she's gotten better with it. She's told me that sometimes her insecurities still get the best of her, but she's learned to talk it out with him. Isabella has always seemed to be better about Finn stripping. She says that it's because he hasn't given her a reason to doubt him. But I know my sister and I think she's just as insecure as Luciana. She just hides it better.

"You have a goofy smile on. I'm guessing you just talked to Maeve." Luciana laughs as she comes over to me.

"Shush." I tease as I put her in a headlock.

"Ewww. I don't want to smell your armpits." She laughs more, pretending she's gagging.

"Maeve and Saoirse are finally moving here."

"SERIOUSLY?" She's jumping up and down.

I love my sister so much. Luciana and I have always been close, and Isabella and Celestino are a duo. When we were little, my parents told us we had to protect our sisters, so Celestino and I agreed that we would each watch one.

"Yes. She said a month, she has to get her shit packed. Callum will be here in a few months too."

"Are you okay with that? I mean truly okay?"

"Yeah, I'm really okay with Callum. I can't be mad at him, he didn't do anything to me. And he took care of my girls when I didn't."

She smiles. "I like Callum, and I'm glad you're okay with him. I don't get the feeling he'll cause problems with you and Maeve. It really seems like he wants what's best for her and Saoirse. Which shows he's a good person because he's not willing to just leave her."

"I agree, and seeing him with Saoirse, I don't think it would be good for her to be ripped away from him."

"Mam and Papà are going to be so happy. I think you should offer one of the prospect houses to Callum. That way he can be close to everyone."

Trust my sister to think of things that I wouldn't.

"That sounds like a great idea. I'll mention that to Maeve, I think it will make her happy."

Chapter Twelve

Francesco

There's only one day left before my girls are here in Chicago. I've never been so nervous about anything before. Not even performing makes me feel like this. Maeve says she's okay with me stripping. But she's never been to a show, so that's another worry for me. At least my sisters will be there with her.

It's time for our nightly call and after talking to Saoirse, I tell Maeve what Luciana suggested. With all my worries that she would change her mind about moving, I forgot to tell her till now.

"I was talking to Luciana and she suggested that Callum might like living in one of the

houses on our property. That way he can still be close to Saoirse."

"That sounds perfect, I'll tell him. He was just saying how he had to look for a place to live. It was worrying him, because he won't be working."

"He won't have to pay anything if he stays in one of our places. Make sure he knows that."

"I will. Thank you, Franco. This means a lot. I know Saoirse will be happy that she can go visit him."

I'll do anything to make this move easier on my girls. Even having Callum live next to us. I hear her laughing and it makes my heart happy. She's leaving her home behind to make a life with me. The least I can do is make sure Callum is happy here too.

"Callum told me that he's interested in Moira. I saw them talking and looking cozy with each other when we were in Scotland."

"I heard her saying that she was interested in him when she was talking to Luciana. But

she's worried that you won't like it. She said something about a girl-code thing."

"Girl code? What's a girl code?"

"My love, do you really think I know what that means?"

We both start laughing

"Well you might?"

More laughing from her.

"You're crazy, baby. I don't understand half of what my sisters talk about. All I know is she said you don't break girl code, and that because you're moving here, you're part of their tribe."

"I've never really had girl friends. In fact, any friends were hard to find."

I hear sniffling. Fuck. I can't have my girl crying.

"It's okay, piccola lontra you have lots of them now. And they're as loyal as the rest of the family."

"Thank you for that, Franco. You don't know how good it feels to know Saoirse and I have you and them too. And thank you for embracing Callum, I know that it hasn't been easy for you."

"I love you Maeve, there's nothing I wouldn't do for you or our daughter. I know It's late there, get some sleep and I'll see you tomorrow. I can't wait to have you both in my arms."

"I love you too. One more sleep and we'll be together again."

After we hang up, I feel good. Who would've thought that inviting Maeve's ex to live on our property would make me happy.

I can't wait for my girls to get here. My sisters and their friends volunteered to start decorating Saoirse's room the day she told me she was coming. Because I have no idea how to do that, I agreed. I'm still worried about how Maeve will react when she comes to our shows. And then she'll still have to deal with me doing private shows.

I text Rónán. I'm hoping he will have some advice on how to show Maeve she can trust me no matter what those women do.

Francesco: Hey man, you busy? I have a few questions

Rónán: I got time, what's up?

Francesco: How did you get my sister to understand that you don't want the women we dance for? Maeve is nervous about all that and I don't know how to help her

Rónán: That's a hard one. Since she's been involved in the business from before we met and she's at all the shows, so she knows what goes on. But I don't do solo privates anymore. Only duo or more. It's not that she doesn't trust me, I feel like it just makes her feel better knowing I'm not alone with the women

Francesco: That's a good idea. I was wondering why you didn't do solos anymore. Lol. So no solo privates, there's enough guys to take care of those anyway. Do you advertise that on our website?

Rónán: Yup. I had Luciana put that on my bio. Only available for duos or more

Francesco: Okay, I'll ask her to put that on mine too

Rónán: It still took a little time. Especially after the shit with Patricia

Francesco: Yeah, I get that. I know it's going to take time with Maeve. But I want to make it as easy on her as I can

> Rónán: I get it. If you want, I'll let Luciana know that you want to change your bio

> Francesco: I appreciate it. Thanks

> Rónán: No problem

I wish there was a fool-proof way of making things easier for Maeve. But I think it's just going to take time. I'm so nervous to have her come to the shows.

Maeve

We're leaving for Chicago today and I'm a nervous wreck. Saoirse is so excited to see her da lontra, but I can see that she's sad to leave Callum too. But she knows that he'll join us as soon as he can.

"Is it time to leave, Mam?" Saoirse giggles.

I laugh. "What day is it?"

"Um. TIME FOR AIRPLANE!" She yells as she bounces around the room.

I laugh while I watch her zoom around like an airplane. She stops in front of Callum.

"You be okay, Da?" she asks him.

He kneels down in front of her. "I'll be okay, and it won't be long before I'm in Chicago."

She hugs him tight. This is the part I hate, both

Saoirse and Callum are sad. Leaving Callum behind is hard. But I know this is what I need to do.

I've almost got everything packed, just the last few items that we've been using and I'm done. Part of me is sad to leave Ireland, it's the only home I've ever known. Callum's mam and grandparents said they'll visit my parents' and nana's graves for me. And his grandparents said they're coming to visit us in Chicago after Callum moves. I think they're all having a hard time with him leaving. It makes me sad knowing that they're hurting too. Fiona has already booked her flight, she'll be coming over in a few months.

"I don't like waiting. It's yearssss." She's been very dramatic lately which can be amusing, yet frustrating.

"It's not years. It's one day."

She makes a weird noise, then runs out of the room. Which gives me time to look around and make sure I'm not leaving anything behind. Callum will mail anything I'm leaving behind, but he's already doing so much that I don't want to forget too many things.

"I'm going to miss both of you so much," Callum says from the doorway.

"We're going to miss you too."

I'm a crier. I cry at almost everything and looking at Callum makes the tears I was holding back come flooding out. He comes over and hugs me.

"Don't cry, Maeve. It's all going to work out the way it should. I know it."

"I hope I'm not making a huge mistake by moving so soon."

"Love is never a mistake. No matter how many chances you take on it. Francesco didn't cheat on you. So I know you can find your way back to each other."

Callum is a romantic, I think that's part of what drew me to him. Even after not having his da in his life, he still believes in love. He believes that there's someone for everyone. But you have to be open to finding it. He told me that his mam dates but because of whatever his da did to her, she's always been afraid to truly let someone in. I told him maybe his da was her one true love, but he says if that's the case, why would he have left them? I think sometimes there are circumstances that make decisions for us. Look at Francesco and me, just because he left me before, doesn't mean we aren't soulmates. It just wasn't our time yet.

"I hope you and Moira are happy too. I can't wait for you to finally be here with all of us."

"Me too. Even if it doesn't work out with Moira, I'll still be around." He smiles.

"I wouldn't have it any other way."

I let Callum know about the conversation I had with Franco last night about him living on the property.

"Are you sure he's okay with that?" he asks me.

"Of course I am. Are you? You're the one that's uprooting your whole life."

"It sounds really nice. To be able to have everyone around, I won't be alone. I'm also excited to see the club and all the members. The way Franco and his family talk about them, they're all really good people. Maybe they'd let me prospect?"

I smile at him. "I'm sure they would. The Cimaruta would be lucky to have you as a member."

"I think after I get settled in, I'll talk to Giacomo and see what he thinks. I've enjoyed hanging out with the club members here. The only part that I've noticed is most of them aren't in relationships. Is it because it's hard to have one with that life?"

"My da loved being with the Cimaruta, and he made it work with my mam. Look at Giacomo and Caitríona, they've been together since they were teenagers. When Franco and I started dating, I asked Caitríona how they did it. How she was able to trust Giacomo with all these women throwing themselves at him. Back then, I was worried that Franco might cheat on me. There are women–they call them bunnies–that hang around the club and sleep with whoever wants them. I saw it happen within my da's club and I hated it. She told me it's up to the man. He makes the choice to stay faithful or to cheat. Her da and Giacomo's da never strayed from their wives. You've met them, they've *never* cheated. If you want Moira and the club, you can do it too."

He nods at me and smiles. "I've never been a cheater and I won't start now. I was just worried that sleeping with the bunnies was part of being a prospect."

I shake my head no. "When my da prospected, he was already with my mam."

"That does make me feel better. And I did talk to Moira about the club and she loves being around them too. She said it took a couple of years for Luciana to invite them to the barbecues but now they're all family."

"That sounds about right. The club is selective about who hangs around. I've seen men and women thrown out of barbecues because they either weren't invited or thought they could cause trouble."

"And do all the women have bodyguards?"

"Well, Caitríona, Isabella and Luciana do because they're council members and also the president's family. I'll probably have one too because I'm with Franco. And when Celestino finds his love, she will too."

"That makes sense. Will you be in danger being with Franco? I never really thought about their bodyguards. They just blend in like part of the family."

"No, I don't think I'll be in danger. And that's how they want it. Amante, Ombra and Azrael are also on the council, plus they've been members for a long time. So basically they are family to them."

"I do like that they don't stand out, it doesn't draw unwanted attention to them. I wish I could be your bodyguard. I hate to think that you could get into any kind of trouble. Especially after what Luciana went through recently. That's fucking scary."

"I know it is, but I'll be okay. I doubt Saoirse or I will be left alone much. And Luciana? It can happen, but you also know how hard they worked to get her home. I think being a part of the Cimaruta, it's just something you have to be aware of. But stuff like that doesn't happen very often."

He sighs at me. "Just promise me you'll be safe."

"Always, Callum."

Chapter Thirteen

Maeve

Seeing Franco and the whole Bastianini clan at the airport was a surprise. They are all holding signs, some are hilarious. Luciana's reads 'Looking for the little girl who loves otters'. Franco's reads 'My heart is finally home'.

All the nerves I felt on the plane disappeared when I saw them waiting there for us. It took us a while to get our hugs from everyone, then we headed to the baggage claim area to get our bags. On the drive to the property, I started to remember all the things I loved when I would visit Chicago. I can't help but smile at all of it.

"Are you ready for your surprise?" Luciana asks Saoirse.

"I have a surprise? I love surprises!" she giggles as she jumps up and down.

We follow Luciana to a door that says 'SAOIRSE'.

"That's my name! Is this my room?" she looks up at Luciana.

"Yes, amore. Everything behind this door is for you," she smiles at her. "Okay, are you ready?"

"I'm ready!"

Luciana opens the door. What we see is something out of a dream. The room has her name painted on the wall with otters and a pong. There's a princess castle bed with a slide right in the middle of the room. Saoirse is running up to every stuffed animal she sees and giving them a hug. I can't help the tears that are falling as I watch her.

"Thank you so much, aintin!"

"It wasn't just me. It was aintin Isabella, Franco, and the whole club. They helped put everything together for you. And you have a stuffed friend from each member of the Cimaruta family."

Saoirse's eyes get big as she goes over to everyone in the room and says her thank-you's and gives each one a hug. This family is everything to me.

"Thank you so much." I say. "This is more than I could have wished for."

"You're family. You and Saoirse." Isabella hugs me.

I'm finally home.

Saoirse and I have been in Chicago for a couple of weeks now. Callum will be coming in about a month. He couldn't leave Ireland when we did because he has the cafe to worry about. He hired three managers to run the cafe, and he wanted to train them and be sure that they could handle it. Callum calls Saoirse every day to say hi to her. She still calls him 'da' which I know bothers Franco, but there's really nothing we can do about it.

Tonight is the first night I'll be going with Franco to work. I've seen the videos that are posted of his shows. I still don't know if I can handle the it. He's also told me that no one knows they own Magic Nights Chicago. They keep it quiet because they don't want the guys to feel like they weren't even when it came to making money. I asked Luciana and Isabella how they deal with their men dancing. They both said sometimes it can be hard. But you have to remember that it's a job, they don't actually want the women that are throwing themselves at them. I guess we'll see how I feel after tonight. Because I know that I could never ask Franco to stop, he loves it so much.

We arrive at the club a few hours before it opens.

Franco wants me to see his routines beforehand, he thinks it'll help me feel better later on. I'm doubting it will help—I don't want any woman's hands on my man.

I stand with the girls as the guys get ready to run through their routines in the order they'll perform tonight. I can see now why the shows are always sold out. Holy hell, they're all sexy. Now, I know who my heart belongs to, but I would be lying if I said all the other guys weren't drool worthy.

It's finally Franco's turn, and he takes me onto the stage with him. You can hear the women in the audience groan. I'm guessing they were hoping he would pick one of them instead. He's only just begun and I'm already wet. I've never had much self-control with him and watching him dance is making it worse. I'm not sure I can wait till we get home to have him inside me. Maybe there's a closet...or his dressing room?

The show was a lot of fun. Franco made sure to bring me up for each of his three songs. I know that's not something he can do every night, but it made me feel better. Somehow I even fought my urge to jump him after each performance. Go me!

Now the after party is another story. He has to mingle with the people who came to the show. There are separate areas, VIP and regular. The VIPs pay extra to be able to meet the dancers. The guys go into the regular area every once in a while. When I asked Celestino about it, he said they do it to show that even if the patrons can't pay the extra money, they're still important.

"How are you doing?" Bella asks as she hands me a drink.

"I'm doing okay..." I trail off as we see a woman walk up to Franco and put her hand on his arm. She needs to get her slimy hand off of him...that arm is mine, dammit. I can see the anger on his face and then he motions to Amante and Ombra. They are Luciana and Isabella's bodyguards.

"It does get easier," Luciana says to me while Bella nods. They turn their heads to see what I'm staring at.

"What the fuck is she doing here?" Luciana growls.

"Who is she?" I ask her.

"Someone who isn't supposed to be anywhere near anyone or any property with the Bastianini name."

"Is she Franco's ex?" I don't know if I really want the answer but I had to ask.

"No!" All the girls answer at once.

"She's a psychopath who thought she was in a relationship with Franco. He has a restraining order on her. She started stalking him and showing up everywhere we were. Mam and Papà were getting worried for his safety and ours. So he got the restraining order. Apparently it's not working, though," Bella explains.

"Should I be worried? I mean would she hurt me or Saoirse?"

"No, you don't have to worry."

She doesn't sound sure when she says that but I nod slowly. It looks like Franco and I have something to discuss tonight. I don't want to worry about some psycho woman coming after me because she wants my man.

I look around me and see all the girls. There are seven of us–Isabella, Luciana, Evangeline, Clara, Moira, Quinn and me. Since I moved to Chicago, they have all embraced me and Saoirse like we've been here forever. I've never had girlfriends, most girls I know are always competing with each other for one reason or another. Even when they say they support women. But with Luciana and Isabella's friends? There's no competition or jealousy between them. They're not trying to outdo each other, they truly support one another and I love it.

I've gotten to know Moira since moving here and I think she's perfect for Callum. I can tell she really likes him. She asked me if it was okay for her to talk to him and get to know him. I told her how happy that made me, that all I want for Callum is for him to be happy. She told me that if I felt weird about it at all, she wouldn't because dating your friend's ex is frowned upon. I told her about how Callum came into my life and she knows the relationship between him and Saoirse. I think that made her fall harder for him, I explained to her that I always knew he wasn't *the one*. But that our connection was strong enough to make me want to be with him. Now that Francesco and I are back together, I see more clearly how Callum and I were missing that connection.

"I'm not sure this will get easier to watch," I grumble to Luciana.

Her chuckles make me frown more. I don't know how she and Bella deal with this crap. Women are grabbing the guys' asses and touching them. Okay fine, they're dressed, but does that really make it better? I'll answer that. No. It doesn't. Watching another woman put her hands on your man is never something that's easy to watch. Even when you know he won't cross lines.

"Okay maybe it doesn't get easier. But you do get used to it. There are always women who don't care that the guys are in relationships. But you'll meet a lot of women who do respect the fact that they're with us. Those are the ones that make me feel better about Rónán dancing."

"Stripping, Luciana. Stripping," Eva teases.

"Shush. Dancing sounds better." Luciana chuckles.

I sigh. "I know you're right, Luciana. But it's just so damn hard to watch. I want to go over and smack them."

Now all the girls are giggling at me. They're mean. I stick my tongue out at them, which only makes them laugh harder. Then I squint at all of them, focusing on Moira.

"A little birdie told me that Callum is considering dancing when he moves here."

The look on Moira's face is priceless. I snicker.

"You lie. H-he wouldn't," she stutters out.

The girls start laughing more.

"He *is* sexy Mo, what did you think he was going to do when he moves here?" Bella teases her.

"I actually didn't really think about it. I was just excited that he's moving here." She laughs. "You need to tell your little birdie that Callum won't strip."

I laugh more. "That's what you think."

I love how excited Moira is that Callum is moving here. It's making it a little easier on Franco. I think he was worried for a while that Callum was moving here for me.

Francesco

Tonight went really well. I was so worried that Maeve would hate being here. After I finish school, maybe I'll stop stripping. Maybe. I really love what I do, it's not because of the women, I love performing and spending time with the guys. My twin and I built this business from the ground up. When we started, it was just the two of us. Now we have twenty dancers, including the four O'Callaghan brothers, and five more that are auditioning this week. It's been a wild ride. We don't advertise that we own Magic Nights and Luminescence. Celestino and I agreed when we started that if we did get the business to grow, we wouldn't let that out. We felt that it made the friendships and atmosphere better. This way the guys that work for us don't feel like they have to be cautious around us cause we're the 'boss'.

Watching the look on Maeve's face while I performed was so fucking sexy. When I perform, I never get aroused. But tonight? Holy fuck. My dick didn't get the memo to behave. The look in Maeve's eyes made me want to take her right there. That would never happen though because no one will ever see my Maeve naked except me. I'm definitely going to have fun practicing with her at home.

I used to love the after-party part of our shows. Seeing how much fun all the people were having was always a highlight for me. That was before Maeve came back. Now all I want is to spend time with her. But this is my job. As I stare at my girl talking with my sisters and our friends, I feel a hand on my ass. I step back and see a face I hoped I'd never see again.

"Hey, lover," Tabitha whispers in my ear.

"What are you doing here? The restraining order says you're not allowed near me or this club."

The sound she makes sounds like a pig snorting. "Don't be ridiculous. I know you want me. Why else would your security let me in?"

"That's bullshit. None of my brothers would let you in on purpose. I know you snuck in and if you don't fucking leave, I *will* call the cops."

This crazy-ass woman needs to leave. I wave to Amante and Ombra. Having them here is not only to protect my sisters, but they help with security too.

"Get her the fuck out of here. And if she makes a scene? Call Salvatore."

Salvatore Mancini is part of the Mancini Mafia family and he's also a police officer. On or off duty, he's the one we call when we have problems like this.

"Got it," Ombra answers as he takes Tabitha's arm.

"Get your fucking hands off me!" she screams.

It's a good thing the music is so fucking loud that only the ones close to us can hear her screeching. The guys keep walking her out and make sure the security we have at the door knows not to let her back in. She shouldn't have been in here in the first place, fucking new security. We've been toying with hiring security for the club so that my MC brothers would have more time to be on the floor watching what's going on. But this is why I never wanted to outsource our security.

This is the first night of trying out this new security team and I definitely need to have a talk with whoever was at the door. There are pictures up at the podium with names that show who's not allowed in. So if they're letting people in that shouldn't be in here, fuck that. I'll find another security firm to work with. Or we'll figure out how to do it ourselves. Salvatore has suggested we hire off-duty and retired police.

I met Tabitha almost two years ago at a private show. She kept asking me to go out with her, acting like she was teasing, but she wouldn't stop. Even when I turned her down every time. Then she started showing up at our club and other places we would frequent. I should've known she was trouble. A moment of stupidity plus too much alcohol, and I woke up in her bed. It was a night I don't even remember, but regret to this day. She started stalking me after that, coming to every show we have at the club. She knows where I live, but has never been on the property. Everyone in the MC has made it a rule to never bring women onto the property. We have a few reasons for that. One is because you never know who's crazy and who's not. Another is because we live on the same property as our club and family. So we always get a hotel room if we have a night out.

I finally had to get a restraining order after six months of her showing up everywhere I was. She didn't just show up at the club, she showed up at the gym, dinners, privates. You name it, somehow she was there. She was also telling people that we were engaged. I haven't seen her in over six months and I thought she finally gave up. But here she is. Fuck.

"I told Anthony, one of the owners of the security company, that we need to talk to him after we close up tonight. He's at the door now, but he said he had another employee working it earlier. I told him that's no fucking excuse for her being in here," Amante says to me.

"Thanks. I want you and Ombra in on the meeting with him. And tell Anthony to call the other guy back in too. I want to talk to both of them. Because apparently he employs people who don't fucking pay attention or follow directions."

Amante nods. "Maybe we need a new company. Or hell, just bring the prospects in to man the door. At least we know we can trust them."

I sigh cause he's right. That was our plan before, but we decided on a security team. Wrong fucking choice.

"I'll ask my papà to call church on Monday. We'll get the prospects in for it. I might need you and Ombra too. But I hate to do that cause you need to guard my sisters. Fuck!"

"It's okay. We'll work it out. It's a little easier here in the club, Rónán and Finn are here, so they can help out if we're on the door. And the Mancinis are prospecting, they'd be a good option."

"Thanks, Amante. We'll figure it out, because you're right, we should keep this in the family. It's not working having outsiders involved."

We walk over to our group. Wrapping my arms around Maeve, I breathe her in. I know she saw what happened, but I'm not sure what she was told about it.

"Is that woman a danger to us?" she asks me.

"I don't know the answer to that, but I promise to tell you about her when we get home. But you will have a guard from now on. I'm not sure who yet, but you'll have one by Monday."

She nods at me and lays her head on my chest. At least she doesn't seem mad about it. And she knows the MC life, so having a bodyguard isn't something weird to her.

Chapter Fourteen

Francesco

The rest of the weekend went by without any more drama from Tabitha. I'm not letting my guard down just yet, though. My gut is telling me this is far from over. And I'm not sure what she'll do when she realizes I have a family now.

I asked my papà to call church, just council members first. I want to make sure they know about Maeve and Saoirse. And I need to ask one of them to be her guard. This is a normal part of our club life. My sisters bodyguards—Amante and Ombra, are enforcers for the club. Azrael—our road captain, is my mam's bodyguard. Amante grew up with all of us kids and he was someone my parents knew would always take care of Luciana. After this meeting, I want to have the prospects in so we can discuss the security issue at Luminescence.

Since my sister was kidnapped, my papà has added to our council. We went from having ten council members to thirteen, with fourteen prospects as of right now. With our growing family, we wanted to have enough in the inner MC to be able to protect not only the council women, but the children and club members.

My papà hits his gavel on the table.

"Bestia has requested this meeting to discuss a few issues we thought were taken care of, but apparently not. Bestia, the table is yours."

"Thank you, Forza. As you all know, my woman, Maeve and our daughter, Saoirse, are now living with me here in Chicago." The room gets loud with hoots and cheers.

"Exactly, it's the best thing that has happened to me in a long time. But now I have a problem. That woman, Tabitha Cross. Some of you will remember her from last year when she was stalking me, and I ended up having to get a restraining order. Well she's back, and if it was just me, I could handle it. But it now involves Maeve and Saoirse. So anyone at the gates needs to make sure she's never allowed through. I'm asking for one of you to be Maeve's bodyguard. And I need someone to be with Saoirse when she's in school. I don't need you to live with us like Amante and Ombra do with Fuoco and Dolce. But I do want you in one of the houses close to us on the property."

Everyone at the table starts to talk to each other.

"I know I'm asking a lot because she's not my wife yet. But know that she will be."

"I'll be Maeve's bodyguard." The voice that volunteers is Romano 'Fantasma' Vietti. He's been with our club for about six months now, since he transferred from our charter club, Silenziatori MC, in Rome, Italy.

I nod at him. "Grazie, I appreciate this."

"I already live close to you so I will not have to move," he says in his thick Italian accent. "Will I be protecting the little one too?"

"I'll take care of the princess." We all turn and look at Granchio. He's been with us for ten years now.

"Thank you," I say to both of them. "I can't express how much this means to me."

"And I don't have to move either. I live near you and Fantasma," Granchio says.

This is one of the best parts of being in our club. The family we've created and how each and every one of us is willing to help the others, no matter what is being asked.

"Other than that, my only worry is Tabitha. She's delusional and still under the impression that we're together, somehow."

"That will teach you to pay better attention to where you stick your dick." Hollis 'Cavallo' Taylor, another of our enforcers, laughs.

"Fuck off," I growl at him. Asshole.

"We've all done dumb shit before," Ombre says, coming to my rescue.

"Not me," Dolce says as she bats her eyelashes. "I always know what I put in my shit. And who it belongs to."

My papà whips his head around to face Dolce. "Was that really necessary?" He frowns at her.

"Sorry." She giggles. "I was feeling left out. Why should they have all the fun just cause they're guys?"

"I think I need some bleach for my brain," Giustizia grumbles as Dolce laughs even more and Fuoco is snickering.

"I think this meeting is getting off track," Forza says as he glares at my sisters. "Let's get the prospects in here for the next part."

We wait for Fantasma to round up the prospects. With so many new prospects, the room fills up quickly.

"I want to make sure everyone is on the look out for Tabitha. I don't know if she'll stop at harassing me. She could go after anyone she sees near me. Or anyone wearing the Cimaruta cut," I say, passing her picture around. "That's the picture the cops gave me to pass out. Memorize that bitch and don't let her get near you."

Everyone nods in agreement, I know if there's any group of people I can trust besides my blood family, it's my club. Besides my papà, Cavallo and Granchio are the longest members.

My grandfathers, Pietro and Liam come over from Italy and Ireland together, wanting a better life for their children. My grandparents lived their lives their own way, that included making sure that Pietro's son married Liam's daughter. Luckily my parents were soulmates. The story they tell is that they were close as children, my papà said he always felt the need to protect my mom. When they became teenagers, my mam went on a date with a boy from their school. My papà said he followed them the entire night and realized that he couldn't stand seeing her with someone else. That was the first and last date my mam went on that wasn't with my papà.

My papà prospected when he was seventeen, my Nonno Pietro was president and my Granda Liam was his vice president. When my grandfathers were ready to step down and go back to their countries, my papà was voted in as President. They went back to their countries and started Cimaruta charters in Italy and Ireland.

"Tabitha got into the club on Friday night and caused a bit of trouble. I know Maeve is worried about her," Fuoco adds.

"How did she get in the club?" Forza asks.

"We were trying out that new security company. One of their guys let her in after she blew him." Celestino frowns.

"I hope you fired that company."

"Right after we closed," I say.

My papà nods his head. "Good. We don't need anyone working with us that can't keep his dick out of his decisions."

"Don't worry, Maeve won't be alone from now on," Fantasma says.

"And Saoirse will be safe too," Granchio chimes in.

"I also want to set up a schedule for all the prospects to be part of the security at Luminescence," I say as they all nod. "Some of you are part of the show, so of course you can't be security too. But I would like the rest of you to help out."

"I'll come up with a sheet for everyone to sign up," Dolce says. "If you can't do a whole shift, it's okay, I'm sure we can work it out between everyone here now and our other members."

"Okay, let's keep our eyes and ears open for this lunatic, Tabitha. No one goes anywhere alone. Everyone in pairs, guards on their highest alerts. Meeting adjourned." My papà hits his gavel and we all stand to leave.

"Thank you for stepping up to help my family," I say to Fantasma and Granchio.

"Your family is my family too. I haven't had the privilege of finding the right woman for me. I'm honored to help you protect yours," Fantasma answers.

Granchio nods. "Family, brother."

When church is over, I head home. Before Maeve

and Saoirse came to live with me, I would've stayed at the clubhouse and hung out with my club brothers. I was never into fucking the girls that hang around, they still try but it's not what I like to do. Knowing that they've been with my brothers makes me cringe.

Now I can't wait to get home to my girls. I know Maeve has been struggling with what she wants to do now that's she's here. I'm trying to be supportive and not push her to do anything she doesn't want to do. My parents offered to take care of Saoirse if Maeve wants to work or go back to school. Saoirse will be starting preschool in a couple of weeks and she's so excited.

I've also been talking with the otter conservation group here in Chicago. My plan is to have a family of otters come and live on the club property. We have a few ponds so they're making sure that it's suitable for them to live here. They came out last weekend to do a final check of the ponds and surrounding areas. I'm hoping to hear back from them this week. I'm very excited about having an otter family live here. I haven't told Maeve or Saoirse, I want it to be a 'Welcome to Chicago' surprise.

Maeve

After what happened on Friday night with that Tabitha woman, I'll admit I'm a little worried. Franco told me all about her. While I think he did a stupid thing, shit happens. What worries me is that he doesn't remember having sex with her. Just waking up next to her.

They also ended up firing the security company because the guy who was at the door admitted he let her in because she 'sucked him off'. Those were his exact words according to Franco. Who knows what else he would have let slide if she'd offered him more. I did hear the owner of the security company asking Franco for another chance, but Franco and Celestino said no. The security of the club and the people in it is the most important thing to them. And one fuck up is more than enough. I admire them for sticking to their guns. They don't take chances or provide sub-par security.

I've also been given a bodyguard–his name is Romano 'Fantasma' Vietti, an enforcer for the MC, and Mitchell 'Granchio' Harris will be with Saoirse at all times. It does make me feel better having them around, and knowing I won't have to worry about Saoirse when she's in school is a relief.

Even though I feel better having the guys with us, I still have a bad feeling about this Tabitha woman. Like that ominous feeling of something bad is coming–when the hairs stand up on your arm, but you don't know why. Franco says I don't have to worry so much, because everyone is on high alert. But Franco has a restraining order, and she got around it. More than once. She doesn't care, she thinks she's above the law.

This weekend went okay, I guess. I'm still not comfortable watching women put their hands on my

Franco. But I agree with Luciana and Isabella when they say no matter how much it bothers them, they would never tell Rónán or Finn that they don't want them to dance. And I would never tell my Franco not to either. Watching him do his routines, I see how happy he is while he's performing. He makes sure that the women keep their hands where he puts them. There were a few women who got up onstage but weren't allowed to stay up there because they couldn't keep their hands where the guys put them. Even the single guys make sure the women know they can't just touch them wherever or whenever they want.

I'm not sure what I'm going to do now that we're in Chicago. Luciana suggested I apply to Wolf and go for my degree. I've always wanted to be a veterinarian. Franco's mam and da have offered to take care of Saoirse if I decide to do that. Getting that degree and becoming a veterinarian would be a dream come true.

Chapter Fifteen

Maeve

It's now been three months that Saoirse and I have been here in Chicago. Franco and I have had a few minor issues, but for the most part, things have been great. In fact, better than I dreamed they would be.

Every weekend we spend time with the club or just the three of us. We go for drives to show Saoirse her new home and to the aquarium and the zoo's. Franco has made this transition easy for both of us. Plus, he's been doing everything he promised, and more.

Callum arrived last month, and he and Moira started seeing each other right away. They're so happy together and I love that he's found his person. And it makes me even happier that it's Moira. She's still worried about this girl code thing which makes me laugh. I suppose if I thought Callum was my soulmate, I'd be mad. But he's not and I'm thrilled he's so happy.

I've decided to go back to school to become a veterinarian. I want to specialize in otters. I have some credits that I earned back in Ireland that Wolf University is allowing me to transfer–just some basic stuff. But it helps, because that means I can dive right into my core classes. Saoirse has settled in so well with the Bastianini clan. She loves everyone so much, and all the MC brothers adore her. She started preschool this week. I was worried that she wouldn't like it, but I was so wrong. She's super excited to get up every morning for school.

"Do you think Saoirse will ever call me d'a'?" Franco asks me as we lay in bed waiting for her to wake up.

"I do think she will, maybe you could tell her that if she wants to, she can? We've never really talked to her about names."

"She knows I'm her da, but she doesn't call me 'da.' And I do like Callum but hearing her call him 'da' kills me."

"Do you think if she called you 'da' it would hurt less?"

"I do. It's not the fact that she calls him that. It's the fact that she doesn't call *me* 'da.' I know it sounds stupid. I'm just being petty."

"You're not being petty. I understand why it hurts."

It's breaks my heart to hear how much Franco is hurting over this. But I don't know what to do about it.

He sniffles and sighs. "I'm sorry, amore. I'm just being a selfish asshole. It's my fault she calls Callum 'da.' If I hadn't left you, it would've been me. You would've been with *me*. Not Callum."

"Franco, you're not an asshole. What happened in the past can't be changed. And yes, we agreed that we wouldn't force her to call you da. But telling her that you'd like it if she did when she's ready isn't forcing her."

"Are you sure? It feels like I would be making her feel like because I want it, she'll feel like she has to do it."

"You know how smart our daughter is. Just tell her that you love her and when she's ready, you would like it if she called you 'da.'"

Right as he's about to say something, we hear her little feet running to our door. Then a tiny knock.

"Can I come in? It's morning!" we hear Saoirse calling from the other side of the door.

"Who is it?" Franco calls out.

"It's me!"

"Who's me?"

"MEEEEEEEE!"

We both start laughing.

"I don't know who 'meeeeeeee' is," Franco teases her.

"It's Saoirse Liliana Bastianini!" she says dramatically.

"Ohhhhh! Okay, you can come in, then."

She opens the door, runs to the bed and climbs in with us. "You're silly, Da Lontra." She giggles.

"Saoirse, why do you call Franco, 'da lontra'?" I ask her.

Saoirse scrunches up her little face. "Because he's my da and he's a lontra."

I hear Franco gasp softly when she says he's her da.

"Baby, you know da isn't a lontra right?"

"What do you mean, Mam? We're all lontra's, like the ones that lives in our pond. When I met Da, he called you 'piccola lontra.' You said that meant 'little otter', so that means we're otters."

Listening to our daughter explain herself is amazing. At four years old, she listens and understands so much.

"You're right, love. I do call your mam 'piccola lontra.' Do you know why?" Franco asks her.

"No why, Da?"

Francesco

My daughter called me 'da.' In fact, she's been calling me 'da' from the day we went to see the otters and I didn't even realize it. I thought that she called me 'da lontra' because it was just something to call me. Not because she was really calling me her papà. I'm such a dumbass. I gather her in my arms and hold her.

"I call your Mam 'piccola lontra' because when we

met, she reminded me of the lontras that live at the pond in Ireland."

Saoirse giggles. "See? We are lontras. If Mam's a lontra, then you have to be and I have to be."

The logic of my four year old daughter's mind just blows me away. I start laughing. "You're right, amore. We can be lontras."

"YAY!" she cheers and giggles more. "I brushed my teefs."

"Good job, baby. Now you need to eat breakfast and get dressed. What would you like for breakfast? Pancakes? Cereal?" I ask her.

"Hmmmm. Can we have pancakes? With syrup? The mabel one?"

"You mean maple syrup?"

"Yes!" She giggles.

"Anything for my girl." I scoop her up and we head to the kitchen.

"I'll be right out to help." Maeve chuckles.

While I'm getting everything together to start cooking, I look over at Saoirse and she looks like she has something to say.

"What's the matter, baby?" I ask her.

"Is Callum still my da? Can I still call him that? There's a girl at school that said I can't have two das."

"Of course you can still call Callum 'da.' And that girl is wrong, you can have two da's."

"But she says you can only have one real da."

I have to think about this one before I answer. I promised Maeve and Callum that I was okay with him still being in Saoirse's life. And I am. I don't want her to think she's wrong for calling him 'da' too, he's the da she grew up with.

"Well that's a little harder to explain. But I'll try. I'm what your classmate would say is your 'real' da. And Callum is like your step-da."

Well shit. Going by my daughter's expression, I think I've just made it worse.

"What your da means is this—you're lucky because you have two das. And I promise when you're a little older, we'll explain it more. But right now, all you need to know is that you have two das that love you so very much," Maeve says as she's walking into the kitchen, saving me.

Maeve's explanation seems to satisfy Saoirse. That's a relief because I didn't know what else to say.

"Okay, Mam. Can I see Da Callum today?"

"Of course. You can go after school."

"Yay! Will you come with me, Da?"

"Of course I will," I say, kissing her on the head. "Okay, sit down and eat your breakfast. I'm going to go and get dressed."

It's amazing how hearing Saoirse call me 'da' can make me feel so good. I still wish everyday that I hadn't fucked up and left Maeve. I missed so much with my girls. And I know that I have time to make up for it. But all the time in the world can't take away how much I missed already.

"Don't forget, Granchio will stay with Saoirse from now on while she's at school. And Fantasma will be with you now that you're back in school," I say to Maeve as we wait for Saoirse. She insisted on getting dressed by herself today.

"Are you sure Granchio is okay hanging out with a four year old?"

I chuckle. "Yes, amore, he volunteered to do it."

Maeve comes over and hugs me. "Thank you for taking such good care of us."

"I will do anything and everything for you two. You're everything to me." I kiss her and we hear a little giggle.

"Kissing again."

I turn and scoop Saoirse up and we squish her between us. I kiss her face and that makes her laugh more.

"You remember Granchio?" I ask Saoirse.

"From the clubhouse?"

"That's right, he's going to be taking you to school from now on."

"Because you and Mam have school too?"

"Yes, amore. And you make sure you listen to what Granchio says, okay? Don't go anywhere with anyone but him."

"Okay, Da. I promise."

We hear a knock at the door. I head towards it, still carrying Saoirse.

"What do we say when someone knocks?" I ask her.

"WHO IS IT?" she yells.

We hear laughing. "It's Granchio, here to take the princess to school."

Saoirse squirms so I put her down, and she swings the door open as she's giggling.

"I'm ready!"

Granchio laughs more. "You look beautiful, princess. Your cage awaits."

"No motorcycle?" She frowns.

"No, sorry. You're too little to ride a motorcycle."

Saoirse pouts at him. "I'm not too little, Da got me one."

"But we had a deal with your motorcycle, remember?" I ask her.

Saoirse frowns at us, then sighs. "Only when you're watching and not outside the gates."

"That's right. Same goes for being a passenger on one. No riding with anyone until your mam or I say it's okay."

"And that won't be for a long long loooong time," Maeve chimes in.

"That's not fair." She pouts even more.

"It's totally fair. In fact, if you keep pushing, you'll lose your motorcycle too," Maeve adds.

"Time to ride in your cage," she huffs to Granchio. He's holding back a laugh as he watches Maeve and Saoirse.

"She's got spunk," he whispers to us.

"Too much sometimes," Maeve says to him.

He laughs. "Okay, let's go, princess. Say bye to Mom and Franco."

"You mean Mam and Da," she corrects him as she comes over to give each of us a hug and kiss.

"You have a good day, baby," I say hugging her.

"I love you, Da."

Those four words make my heart melt.

"I love you too. So much." I hug her tighter.

"Squishing me, Da." She giggles.

I hand over her backpack for school. We watch her skip as she follows Granchio out the door. It's been a great morning.

Chapter Sixteen

Francesco

For the last few weeks, we haven't seen Tabitha. I know she's still following us, and it's making me fucking paranoid. I'm more worried about Maeve and Saoirse. I've talked to Fantasma and Granchio about it and we've brought it up in church. But there's only so much we can do until she crosses the line.

I've added Maeve and Saoirse's names to the restraining order. It helps that we know people that can do these things for us. But like Luciana says, it's really just a piece of paper. We need to be vigilant and make sure everyone is safe. I don't know how much more any of us can take.

Maeve finally decided to apply to Wolf to get her degree. She started last week, I'm excited because that means she's at school when I am. Which means more time to see my girl. And I know my Saoirse will be safe because she has Granchio with her.

"Hey, love," I hear someone say and I feel a hand touch my arm.

"Tabitha. Do you want to go to jail?" I snap at her.

She laughs. "You really think that restraining order can keep me away from you? We both know you want me. And that we'll be together forever."

"Okay. One last time. Listen well because I won't say it again–stay away from me. There's nothing between us. There never was."

"You're a fucking liar. You told me I was the best fuck you ever had. I know you're doing this because of that Irish bitch that's been hanging around you."

"Stay away from her."

Tabitha stares at me. Then gives me a smile that I can only interpret as evil.

I walk away and barely hear her say, "I wonder if this is how you'd be if she wasn't in the picture."

Everything in me wants to turn and threaten her but I know that's not going to help. She wants me to start something.

"I'll see you soon, lover!" she yells at me.

"Well I guess that answers the question of whether Tabitha had given up or not," my twin says as he walks up to me.

"Fuck. I told you I had a feeling she was following me. That damn restraining order doesn't mean shit to her."

"There's got to be something else we can do. Be proactive, because right now she's so far ahead of us and showing up everywhere. It's making all of us fucking crazy."

"And do what? I talked to Salvatore yesterday. He said all we can do is keep calling it in when she shows up."

"That's fucking stupid. You don't think she'd go after Maeve, do you? Has she mentioned Saoirse?"

"Not Saoirse, but she has mentioned Maeve more than once."

"Fantasma and Granchio would never let anyone near them."

"I know that, but we thought we could keep Luciana safe and look what happened."

"That was totally different, bro. T-Rex planned that shit for a while, Tabitha is just a crazy bitch who needs to get a life."

"The crazy ones are the worst, from what Sal said."

Celestino sighs. We both know Sal's right and Tabitha could spiral and do something unhinged. But I don't know what to do about it. How do you get into the head of a psychopath? The more Tabitha shows up, the more crazy she looks.

Maeve

I know Franco is worried about that woman,

Tabitha. He's told me everything that's happened and how he even has a restraining order out on her. But no matter what, she keeps popping up. She's been arrested a few times now for trespassing at the club. But when she shows up in other places, they can't get the police there fast enough to catch her. And when they go to her place to confront her, she denies ever being near him.

Salvatore Mancini is a close family friend. He's a Chicago police officer and he's been trying to help us out. But it feels like until Tabitha does something really drastic, there's nothing we can do.

When my class ends, Fantasma and I head to the place where I meet Franco after each class. I see Tabitha walking towards me, away from Franco and Celestino. What the hell is she doing here?

"You better reconsider being with my man," Tabitha says to me.

Fantasma steps between us.

"Leave us alone." I know I shouldn't engage her, but it infuriates me that she thinks she can call Franco hers.

"Poor little Irish girl needs a bodyguard? You don't know anything. This is a game you're going to lose, little girl," she cackles.

Fantasma makes sure I'm behind him, but the stubborn part of me wishes she would step across that line so we can finally get her for something. I see Franco and Celestino running towards us.

"Keep walking, Tabitha. Or fuck it, stay here, the

cops will be here any minute," Franco says, gathering me into his arms.

"Why would you call the cops? I've done nothing wrong." She smiles at Franco. We hear sirens getting closer.

"Remember what I said," she says to me, then turns and walks away.

"What did she say to you?" Franco asks.

"She told me that you're her man, and this is a game I'm going to lose."

I feel his arms tighten around me.

"That woman is going to cause a lot more trouble," Fantasma says, frowning.

We see Salvatore Mancini and his partner, Mac, walking over to us.

"Everyone okay?" Salvatore asks.

"This time. There's got to be something we can do, Sal. Tabitha doesn't give a shit about the restraining order," Franco growls.

"I know, man. But short of having a police escort everywhere you go, I'm not sure there's anything we can do."

"Fuck that. I'm not having a cop with me 24/7," Franco growls.

Sal sighs. "I know it's not what you want. But the last guy she stalked disappeared. Like I can't find a trace of him anywhere."

"Do you think she killed him?" I ask.

"Either that, or he changed his name and is in hiding," Mac answers.

"Are you serious?"

"Yeah. We did a background check after she started stalking Franco last year. That's how we got the restraining order so fast. We brought that information to the judge and he agreed that Franco could be in danger."

"I want to know more, but I have to get to my next class," I say giving Franco a kiss.

"I'll see you after class, piccola lontra."

I nod and head to class with Fantasma.

Francesco

"Wait, she's got priors?" Celestino questions Sal. "All we heard about was the guy who is hopefully in hiding."

"There's been a few others. She didn't actually do anything to them, but she followed them everywhere. There's reports on it. You sure know how to pick 'em."

"Fuck you, Sal. I didn't pick her. I didn't know that she was a crazy bitch either."

Sal laughs. Asshole.

"Well either way, you shouldn't have messed with her. Wasn't she already stalking you when you went home her?"

"Fuck me. I made a stupid mistake—I was fucking drunk. And I think she might have slipped me something, because I don't remember anything after we closed up that night. Next thing I know, I was waking up in her bed."

"Seriously? Why didn't you report it?"

"Because at the time I just figured I must have drank too much. But when I talked to Luciana, she said I only had a few, and I never told anyone where I was going."

"We usually make it a point to text each other and let the other know what hotel and room number, or at least an address," Celestino explains.

"You should've told me that when we did the restraining order. We could've added that in."

I keep quiet. It's embarrassing enough that I was so dumb as to accept a drink from that psycho. But to wake up in her bed was the icing on that asshole moment. I never heard my phone ring or any of the text messages that came in all night.

"Don't you all have trackers like we do?" Sal asks quietly.

"We do, and we did check Franco's that night. We found the address he was at, but didn't know it was the psycho bitch. We thought maybe he went home with a random woman and forgot to text us. Trust me, we haven't made that mistake again," Celestino says.

"I get it. It happens, but now that we know she's doing this, you need to be alert. You have someone watching your daughter?"

"Granchio is with her."

"Okay good, I'll see what else we can do. Just keep calling when she shows up. And make sure Maeve knows to call too. Give her my number, it's faster if you call me instead of dispatch. Because if it's technically not an emergency, you would need to call the non-emergency line anyway. Unless she threatens you, then you call 9-1-1."

"Okay. Thanks, Sal. We really appreciate your help. I'll make sure Maeve has your number. Let's hope Tabitha gives up soon."

"We can hope. Call me if you need anything."

We say bye to Sal and Mac. I see Tabitha standing in the distance, watching us. Since she's across the courtyard, technically I can't do anything. Fuck. That horrible feeling is back again.

After waking up in Tabitha's bed, I made a conscious decision to never take drinks from any of the customers. And to not leave my drinks on tables or anywhere, really. I wasn't lying when I told Sal I think she drugged me. That was also the last time I was with a woman I didn't actually know. I'm not a saint, but I stopped saying yes to the women that come to the shows.

Chapter Seventeen

Maeve

I keep seeing Tabitha while I'm at school. It feels like she's not only following Franco, but she's following me too. Having Fantasma with me makes me feel safe. I know that when Franco can't help me, Fantasma will. And knowing that Granchio is with my Saoirse, I'm not as worried about her. Not that I'm not worried at all, because I am. I keep expecting Tabitha to show up on the property. I know no one will let her in the gate, but I do wonder why she hasn't tried yet.

Most of the club members live on the property, and there's always someone at the front gate. Which makes me feel safer at home.

"Tabitha is still following us at school," I say to Franco.

"I know, baby, it's frustrating that she's staying just far enough away that we can't do anything. But I guess it's also good because she isn't in your face."

"Seeing her is hard enough. I'm always wondering when she's going to cross the line."

Franco wraps his arms around me. "She's not going to touch you. And if by some slim chance she does? I will make sure that's the last thing she ever does," he whispers to me.

I hold him tight. "I know you will. But I don't want it to come to that."

"She's crazy, but I don't think she's crazy enough to attack any of us."

I sigh softly. I want to believe what Franco is saying but I can't. I *know* she's planning something and I get the feeling it's going to be really bad. I also worry about Saoirse, what if she goes after her?

"I can see the wheels turning in your pretty head. Talk to me."

"I'm just worried. You keep saying that she's crazy but you don't think she'd come after any of us. But I disagree. I think she's going to try something and it's going to be bad. Be honest with me, Franco."

He sighs, then takes a deep breath. "You're right. I do have a bad feeling about it. But we have to let this play out and see what she does."

I frown at him. I know he's right, but that doesn't mean I have to be okay with it.

Francesco

I'm lying to Maeve when I tell her that Tabitha isn't crazy enough to attack any of us. The dread I feel gets worse every time I see her. I have to make sure my family is safe. All my family. At this point, I worry about my parents, siblings and my club. Who knows what Tabitha is really capable of? Sal said they still haven't found the other guy that disappeared. He's been missing for a year now.

I wake up everyday with a sick feeling in the pit of my stomach because I know we'll have to deal with Tabitha. But today? Today I feel like something is really off. And I don't like it. The last time I felt like this, my baby sister was kidnapped.

"I'm not going to my last class today, my professor called it off because he's sick. Should I stay at school and wait for you?" Maeve asks.

"No, I'd rather you come back here."

She frowns at me. "Are you sure? I don't want you to be at school alone."

"I'm sure, piccolo lontra. And I won't be alone. Celestino will be there too."

Maeve finally nods. "Okay, will you text me after your classes?"

"Of course I will, amore."

I kiss her and hold her tight. "Let's try not to worry

so much. I know we're all stressed out. But we have to keep going."

"I know and I'm trying. I just wish she would give up and go away."

"She will, she has to at some point. Let's get going, traffic looks bad today."

After I get out of my second class, I head to the place where we all meet up. I see my brother and Maeve already there.

"Hello, my love," I say as I kiss her.

"Hi." She smiles back at me.

"I brought your bike and parked it next to Giustizia's." Fantasma says.

"Thanks, eyes open today. I haven't seen her, which is good, but weird."

"Don't worry, I got Maeve. We're headed straight to the clubhouse after this."

"Speak of the devil," I hear Luciana say.

Fuck. She *is* here. I was hoping that she had finally given up. But nope, there she is. Stalking us like every other day.

"Don't leave Luciana alone," I say to Amante. He looks at me like I've grown another head.

"I didn't know that was an option." He frowns at me.

"Sorry. Today just feels extra strange."

Everyone nods and watches the crazy bitch.

"I don't understand why she won't give up. I mean, it's not like you're a great catch or anything," Luciana teases.

"Ha ha. I'll have you know I'm an excellent catch. Just ask Maeve." I smile smugly at my sister, who snorts at me.

"Uh huh," she says, making vomit noises. Sisters suck.

"I'm going to have to agree with Ana." She pauses for her own dramatic effect. "But I do I wonder why she won't give up on you." And of course Isabella has to chime in. I look at the rest of the group and they're all snickering. I roll my eyes at them. They all suck equally.

"Well I think you're super hot. And I do get why she won't let go. Besides the fact that she's crazy," my Maeve says, smiling up at me.

"I love you." I kiss the tip of her nose.

"I love you more. We'll find a way to get through this."

"All kidding aside, Tabitha does creep me out," Luciana says. "It just doesn't make sense. It's not like you had a relationship with her. I wonder if anything actually happened between you two. Especially if she did drug you."

It never dawned on me that I may not have slept with Tabitha. But hearing Luciana say that...she could be right. Like when you have too much to drink, good luck getting your dick to cooperate. I wish I knew what really happened that night.

"Shit. I have to get to class." I sigh.

"I'll go with you, Rónán's class is getting out soon and it's next to yours," Luciana says. "We'll wait for you till your class is over."

"Sounds good," I say, turning to Maeve. "Please be safe, baby. I'll text you as soon as I'm done."

"Okay. You be safe too," she says softly. I give her a kiss and watch her leave with Fantasma.

"I hate this so fucking much. There's got to be something we can do," I grumble.

"I know, Franco. She's going to fuck up sooner or later and then we'll get her. Until then, we do what we need to do. I'd like to know how she's always where we are. It's like she's tracking you or something," Luciana says.

Holy shit. Again, my sister thinks of something I didn't.

"You think she could be tracking us?" I ask her.

"But how would she have gotten a tracker on every one of us? She's been showing up where we are too. Not just you and Maeve," Isabella says.

"Maybe on the bikes?" Amante suggests.

"Fuck. I'll call Sal and ask if he can come look at all the bikes. Cages too," Celestino says.

"Thanks. I wish I could blow off class today, but I have a fucking test."

"Don't worry, I got this. I'll stay here and wait with Luciana and Amante. I don't have any more classes today," my twin says.

I nod. "Thanks. I can leave as soon as I finish my test."

"And I just have to turn in a paper and I'll be back too," Isabella says as she leaves with Ombra.

"This fucking sucks. We need to get back to normal," I say.

"We will, big brother. We will." Luciana hugs me and I hug her back. I hate that they're all so worried about me and this whole fucked-up situation.

Celestino

Sitting on a bench waiting for my twin to finish his class, I can see Tabitha across the lawn watching me. It's fucking unnerving and so damn frustrating. Luciana brought up some good points. We don't really know if Franco had sex with Tabitha. And how the fuck is she everywhere we go? I need to call Sal.

"Hello?" Sal answers.

"Hey Sal, it's Celestino. We were all talking earlier and Luciana brought up a couple of things."

"I'm listening."

"First of all, if Franco was drugged, could it be possible that nothing happened between him and that psycho bitch? And if nothing happened, what did she want from him? And second, we need to find out how she's everywhere we are. Could she have trackers on our bikes and cages and is there a way to find out?"

"Yeah, it's definitely possible nothing happened, but the only one that knows for sure is Tabitha. And I can have one of my tech guys go over all your cages and bikes. Just let me know when."

"Maybe tonight? We'll all be on the property, so that would be a good time. We should be home by six."

"Sounds good. I'm off at four, I'll ask my tech guy if he can come with. If not, I can borrow his gear. I'll see you at six."

"Thanks man, I really appreciate this."

"Not a problem. Be safe."

"Everything okay?" Luciana asks as she comes and sits next to me. She's got Rónán and Amante with her.

"Just got off the phone with Sal. He's going to meet us tonight at six to check the cages and bikes."

"If we can figure this part out, maybe we can finally keep her away from us."

"What if this pisses her off more? It could also make her escalate what she's already doing," Rónán says.

"Fuck. I didn't even think of that. But we have to stop her from following us," I say. "So we really have no other option."

I know that Rónán's thinking about when Luciana was taken. Those two days were the worst I've ever had. Not knowing what happened to my sister, or where she was—no one should ever have to go through that. No one. The only reason we found her so quickly is because we all have trackers in us. Yes, *in* us. When my sisters turned sixteen, we were having problems with other clubs because my papà wanted to take our clubs out of guns and drug running.. That didn't go over very well. They said we were traitors and shouldn't be a motorcycle club if we wanted to be law-abiding citizens. My papà disagreed, he believed that we could be better than what we were.

Because of that, our club and all our charter clubs started getting threats from other high-ranking MCs. So the vote was put out there to place trackers in all patched members. Of course, there are some that chose not to, but as of today, ninety-nine percent of all Cimaruta and our charter clubs are chipped. My papà also made changes to our MC council. My sisters and my mam are on our council and some of our charter clubs have followed suit. It's not a requirement but what *is* required is the respect given to each and every charter no matter what path they choose. The only mandatory part is going legit. No more guns and drugs for our clubs. We own businesses and pay taxes. That's not to say we don't have our 'side' businesses, but we're changing for the better.

My papà has also merged some of our business interests with the Mancini Mafia. Their family owns several businesses, including the Legacy Hotel here in Chicago. They also helped us find my sister when she was abducted. Francesco created the program that we use with our trackers, but when Luciana was taken, the kidnappers somehow figured out how to jam the signal. Sebastiano Mancini is the one that helped Franco figure out what was wrong and how to fix it. It's been a very productive merging of families so far.

Francesco

Salvatore is pulling in behind us as we get home. We let everyone know that he's here to check out our bikes and cages.

"Well, better to be safe than sorry, and at least we'll know if she's tracking us. I wish I had thought of it before," my papà says. "I feel like she's been one step ahead of us this whole time."

"That's my fault. I should've come to you when it happened. I was just so fucking embarrassed, I kept it to myself."

"You should know that there are no secrets in this family. No matter what."

We all agree with my papà. He's right–if I hadn't let my pride get in the way, I wouldn't be in this situation.

"Hey guys, this is my best tech guy, Thomas Dixon. He's going to check all the cages and bikes, then do a sweep of the property," Sal says.

"Sounds good, thank you. I'll have one of our other prospects take you where you need to go," my papà says.

"How are things?" Sal asks after Anthony, one of our new prospects, leads Thomas away.

"We saw her today, she was watching us up until we left to come home. I'm sure she knows where we live," Luciana answers.

Sal nods. "I'm sure she does too. But there's no way for her to get onto the property as far as we know, right? All the guys at the gate can be trusted?"

"Well, we did have to deny one prospect a couple

of months ago. But we usually don't have any issues when we deny membership," my papà says.

"Can I ask why you denied him membership?"

"He just didn't fit in with us. He didn't have any respect for women, and he kept doing things that would make the club look bad if he were to become a member," my papà explains.

"We may want to look into him if Thomas finds trackers on the cages or bikes. Especially if it's on all of them. It's one thing if we find them on the ones that are used regularly, but if it's on all of them...well that would mean someone got in here and put them on. And I'm worried about the perimeter. Like our property, yours is really big and you need an updated system. Maybe Franco can work on that with Sebastiano? The one we use for our property works not only for the main area, but for the campgrounds we own too."

"That's a good idea. Franco? Is that something you can take care of? If not, I don't mind hiring Sebastiano to do it," Papà says, looking at me.

"I would like to take that on. I'll call Sebastiano tomorrow and set up a meeting."

"After we update the system, the next step is to see how we can get rid of her. Which may take modifying the restraining order and adding a clause that encompasses all patched members of the Cimaruta."

"You think she'll target everyone?" I ask.

"Well, I wouldn't put it past her. We still can't find her ex, his name is George and his family still calls daily to see if we have any new information. She says he broke up with her and that was the last time she saw him."

"And you don't think that's true?" Maeve asks.

"No I don't. But without any proof, we can't search her place. He never filed any complaints about her. There were five before him that did. But he didn't."

"Holy shit. She's done it to that many men? How is she not in jail?" My mam blurts out.

"The reports were for threatening and stalking. But then she would stop, I'm guessing when she found her next victim. My feeling is that when George decided to cut things off, she went off the deep end."

"How long were they together?" I ask.

"His family says they were together for almost two years, and lived together for the last eight months. He had moved his things out while she was at work and was supposed to talk to her, then head to his parents' house. He never showed up."

"This is insane," Luciana mutters.

"So what you're saying is, until she actually attacks Franco or someone in the family, there's nothing we can do?" my papà snaps. My mam puts her arms around him. "I'm sorry Sal, this isn't your fault. I'm just so damn frustrated."

"I understand, Giacomo. I hate that I don't have any answers for you. Especially after what your family has already gone through. We'll find a way to get her. Right now Mac and I are trying to find George–I think he's the key to all this."

"I feel sad for his family. Imagine not knowing where your loved one is?" Luciana says sadly.

Rónán wraps his arms around her tightly. "I know what that feels like," he says.

We all turn to look at my sister and her fiancé. I hope they find George. I don't know what we would've done if we hadn't found Luciana. Or if we were too late finding her, that would've changed our family and I'm not sure any of us would ever heal from that.

Maeve

All this talk about the man that's gone missing is scaring me. I don't want to lose Franco, I can't lose Franco. I will hunt this bitch to the ends of the earth if she takes him from me.

The second week after I moved here to be with him, he said something had happened to Luciana but that it was her story to tell. I knew that when she was ready, she would tell me, and then Franco and I could talk about it. After hearing what she went through, what they all went through...I don't know how I would've handled that. And Franco. My poor Franco blamed himself for the tracker not working. It was never his fault, but he still feels like there was more he could've done to prevent it.

Last week, Saoirse, Callum and I had our trackers put in.

"Well, I found trackers on all the motorcycles on the property, as well as all the vehicles," Thomas says to everyone. "I haven't taken them off yet. If they go offline and don't move, whoever put them on will know we found them. That could make them escalate even more."

"That was my thought before," Sal says.

"So what are our options?" Giacomo asks.

"I could clone the signal so that not only does it transmit to the original site, but it would transmit here too." Thomas explains.

"That sounds great. I'd like to get Sebastiano in on that," Franco says.

"I'll call him now, I'm sure he won't mind coming over and getting it set up now," Sal says as he steps away to call him.

"Okay so we set this up so we know what they know. But how does that help us? We're already doing as much as we can with security."

"Until we know who's on the other end of the tracker, we can't arrest anyone. But if we can track it, we'll know who's doing this. Plus, when she shows up where you are, that's more proof she's involved, in case the tracker signal isn't going to her," Thomas explains.

"How long do we need to do this?" Franco asks.

"We need at least a week or so of us tracking the signal. I'll put in a work order so we have a paper trail to use if you need to go to court for it."

"Thank you Thomas, we appreciate your help," Giacomo says, shaking his hand.

"I'll give you my cell number as well. I know that Francesco and Sebastiano know what they're doing. But if you need more help or another set of eyes, don't hesitate to call me."

"Again, thank you. We just want this to be over. I do hope you find George," Luciana says.

"Sal's a great cop, if anyone can find him, he will."

"Are you talking about me again?" Sal laughs. "Bastian is on his way, and he's bringing Skye with him."

"Are you two hungry? I was going to get one of the guys to throw some steaks on the grill," Giacomo says.

"Are you sure? Steaks sound delicious." Thomas chuckles.

"Of course. Prospect, can you get the grill going? Make sure there's enough for everyone. Grab some potatoes too."

"Sure thing, Forza," says the prospect, walking out to the yard.

Chapter Eighteen

Francesco

It took a few hours for Bastian, Thomas and I to set up the system to piggyback the tracker signal. It was a little tricky because we didn't want to disrupt the original signal. And we had to make sure our signal couldn't be detected. We also discussed upgrading the security on our club property. We own about a hundred and fifty acres. It's a lot of area to lock down, but it has to be done.

We need to upgrade the security for our businesses as well. Especially Luminescence, because we spend a lot of time there, and I want all of our dancers and patrons to be safe. This whole thing with Tabitha is making shows hard to do. No one knows when she's gonna show up and go psycho on us.

I haven't done any privates since Tabitha started showing up again. Even though I don't do solos, I don't want to endanger any of my dance brothers by doing group privates either. I miss doing private shows, but I know Maeve is worried and this is the only way I know to help her relax a little. I'll go back to doing them eventually.

Even though I changed what I offer on our website, there's always a few bookings asking for me to do solos and full nudity. But I promised Maeve no more, so I decline those and suggest one of the other dancers. I won't break my promises to her ever again.

"Are you busy tomorrow?" I ask Sebastiano.

"I have class in the morning and I usually go to the office after. Did you need help?"

"I was thinking maybe you can meet me at Luminescence and we can go over the security there. I'd like to add cameras. Not in the dressing rooms of course, but maybe so we can see the doors and hallways? That way if anyone gets to the dressing rooms, we can catch them. Also in front of the bathroom doors, not inside, just the outside."

"Yeah, we can do that. I'm out of class around twelve. I can meet you there after."

"Thanks, that's perfect. Call me when you're on your way and I'll head over."

I hate having to look over my shoulder and Tabitha starting this crap again is making me do that. The only good thing is that Saoirse is too young to know what's going on. She thinks it's awesome that she has her own personal bodyguard. Granchio adores her, and I know she's safe with him.

When I get to the club, Sebastiano is already there checking out the system.

"So what do you think?" I ask him.

"The system is good. But we need to update your software and cameras. I want high-def cameras with audio. There's some now that can pan 180 degrees, and the night vision is almost as clear as daytime," he says.

"Sounds good to me, order whatever we need and let me know how much it is. I was thinking, how about alarms or code locks on the interior doors? I want to build a wall that will separate the dressing rooms from the club area. At least that way we won't have to worry about people trying to slip in there."

"Definitely. I'll get everything ordered. Most of it will only take a few days, maybe a week. But if we want some of the specialty stuff, that will take a bit longer. So your guys will just have to keep watch for now. When are you going to have the wall up?"

"We should have it up within a week. We'll start next Monday."

"If you need extra help, I can ask Elio if he has any guys he can spare. For the construction and security."

"That would be awesome. We could definitely use help with both. Thanks."

"Let me call him now, I'm sure he'll want to come down and check the place out too."

I nod. Elio Salvadori is the head of the Southside Mafia. They came to help us when Luciana was kidnapped, so I know they're trustworthy. We've discussed partnering up with them too.

"Elio said he'll meet us in about an hour if that's okay. He's bringing a few of his guys with him."

"Thanks. Maybe they'll be interested in dancing?" I laugh.

"I know Nico and Mario asked about prospecting," Sal says.

Right now all of the Mancini kids are prospecting, along with the O'Callaghan brothers. There's eleven altogether. They joined us at just the right time, considering what's going on right now. And if some of Elio's crew wants to join us, we would definitely bring them in.

We are selective with who we allow to prospect. The first stage of prospecting is the 'hang-around' and that lasts for at least six months before my papà decides whether or not to let them prospect. He just denied one last month. That's the one we think is the mole. But we're not positive.

True to his word, an hour later Elio gets to the club with Carlo Fenati, his consigliere, and Mario Zaccone, one of his capos. After they take a look around, they agree we can get the wall and door up in a week.

"Mario and Carlo will come and help you this week," Elio says.

'Thank you, I really appreciate the help."

"Is your papà busy today?" Elio asks me.

"I don't think so, I'm pretty sure he's back at the clubhouse."

Elio nods at me. "How are things with the girl? The one who's been stalking you. Has she stopped?"

"No. She's still following me around. So far that's all she's doing, but it feels like something's about to go down." I sigh.

"Is she dangerous?" he asks.

"I think she could be. Sal said that she's done this to other men she's dated and one has been missing for a while."

Elio frowns. "That's not good, Franco. You need to be safer—you need more security."

"I'm never alone. I have one of my club brothers with me at all times," I explain.

"I will leave Mario with you too. I don't like this, she sounds more dangerous than we thought."

"I appreciate it, Elio. But you don't have to do that. I know you need your men too."

He shakes his head at me. "If you were my son, you would have several men with you at all times. And I know your papà. If he had more men, you would have more security. Well, I have the security and now you will too."

Elio is the same as my papà, there's no arguing with them when it comes to us kids.

"Thank you. I appreciate this."

Elio steps forward and gives me a hug. Then he heads over to Carlo and Mario to talk with them. I'm a big guy, six-foot three and two-fifty. Mario has two inches and probably fifty pounds on me. He's a monster, and I'm actually relieved that he'll be with me. This whole situation is getting worse and worse.

Chapter Nineteen

Francesco

It took us almost the whole week to install the new wall and door. Then we added the cameras and extra security. I think all the guys feel better having that wall between us and the people who come to the shows. There have been times where women—and men too— have snuck into one of the dressing rooms. Now there's no way for them to do that.

"You know, when I prospected for the Cimaruta twelve years ago, it never even crossed my mind that I would be in a male strip club watching them strip. Never. Not. Even. Once," Granchio grumbles.

I laugh at him. "Well, there's other clubs you can prospect with if you don't like it here with us."

"Asshole." He sighs.

"Can't I just run the the door? That way I don't have to see you or Giustizia or Rónán fucking naked. There's just some things brothers don't need to share."

"Quit your whining, you're the one who said you wanted to help out more." Fantasma laughs.

"I meant like, around the clubhouse. Or even for the princess. But this? No. Just. No."

We all laugh at him as he continues to moan and groan about seeing naked men.

"Besides, we're not fully naked," Keegan says.

Granchio gives him a dirty look."Is that supposed to make me feel better?"

I laugh harder. "Fine, stay at the door for now. But no flirting with the women, I need your eyes on everyone that comes into the club."

He gives me a slightly horrified look which makes the guys laugh.

"No flirting? Why am I being punished?" Granchio moans.

"You get to see every woman coming into the club and you're mad about it?" Mario laughs.

"Some of these women are scary," Granchio says to him.

"You are bigger than these women. I think you can take them." Mario laughs. His Italian accent gets stronger when he's teasing Granchio.

Shaking my head and laughing, I walk back to my dressing room where Maeve is waiting. Mario stays with the guys to see how things are run.

"Amore." I smile.

"Are you worried about tonight?" she asks me.

"I'm always a little worried. But the club is here and helping with security. We also have the new camera system up and running. Bastian is here to supervise."

"I just wish she would disappear. This whole situation is like something out of a movie."

I go over to her and wrap her in my arms.

"I know it's crazy, but at least for now she's just watching us. None of us are ever alone and I think that's what's holding her back."

Maeve sighs. We hear a knock at the door and I go over to open it.

"Did you want to change up the line up? Or just keep it the same as usual?" Rónán asks.

"It doesn't matter to me, do the guys want to switch it up?"

"Yeah, we're thinking about it. Instead of Keegan going first, Finn wants to, and Celestino said he'd like to close out the show."

"Sounds good to me."

We watch Rónán turn and walk out. I know Maeve still has a problem with my dancing, but it's what I love and I don't want to quit just yet.

"Don't worry, baby, nothing bad is going to happen. We have the club doing our security now. I trust everyone that is involved."

"I hope not," she whispers, clinging to me.

"You want to come up onstage with me for one of my songs?"

"I always want to be onstage with you. And not just because I don't want anyone else touching you." She smiles.

"Okay I'll pick you for one," I say, kissing her.

Maeve

I think it's getting easier to watch Franco onstage. Maybe. The insecurities I had at the beginning about him wanting other women are fading. But they're not totally gone and I'll be the first to admit that I still want to rip their arms off for touching my man.

Tonight is no different. The first woman he brought up onstage licked his abs. Licked. Him. Who the fuck does that? I can't even get myself to hug him after that one. Luckily, he takes a shower after that song.

"That was feckin' gross. Who licks a stranger?" I whisper angrily to Luciana.

"You'd be surprised what they do. Some try to shove their hands inside their coverings to pull them off. These shows aren't full nudity, only the privates have that option. So I guess they feel like it's fair game at the shows. And I agree, some of the things they do are really gross," she says

"Franco said he won't do full nudity anymore."

"Rónán stopped doing them when we got together, too. It makes it a little easier to deal with."

"I've seen some of the messages Franco gets from

the bookings. Some are repeat customers and they want the full nudity." I sigh.

"Yeah but Franco respects you and won't do that anymore. Finn doesn't do it either. The rest of the guys still do, but I'm guessing that if they find their person? They'll stop too."

"I guess I can see why women would want the full show. Am I being selfish for not wanting him to do that?"

"No, you're not being selfish, being selfish would be telling Franco to quit dancing. Or to make him feel bad every time he steps onstage. But you're not doing that. No matter how many times I watch Rónán, I still don't want him doing full nudity."

"You and Bella always seem so calm when the guys are onstage. I feel like I'm going to explode every time one of the women puts their hands on him." I sigh.

Luciana hugs me. "I promise it will get better. It was so different before I was with Rónán. I would watch the shows and the women and laugh. But then I met Rónán...that first night I saw him dance? It was so hard to see him up there. Then there's times he comes offstage and even comes home from privates with scratches on him. It makes me want to kill these women for leaving marks like he's theirs."

Knowing that I'm not the only one who has issues with this makes me relax a little more. I've always feel like I'm too uptight and making it harder for Franco. And I don't want to do that. I can see the happiness on his face when he performs and I won't be the one to take that away from him.

Francesco

The after party at the club is always a good time. But tonight feels different. There's something in the air here and it's making the hairs on my arms stand up. I can see my club brothers are on edge too.

"Is it me or does it feel extra off in here tonight?" I ask Granchio.

"Yeah, it felt like that all night. Nothing going on, though. Just a feeling, and I don't like it."

Scanning the crowd, I see some women wearing property cuts of a rival club of ours, the Crimson Royals. They're a club out of California that attacked our club nine years ago. But this is the first time I'm seeing their cuts in our territory. That's never a good sign. I head back over to Granchio. I wish I could see the member's name on the cut, all property cuts say who they belong to.

"See those women with the cuts? Keep an eye on them. You weren't around for it, but the Cimaruta have had problems with that club for a long time. Also keep an eye on Amante. That's the club that killed his papà."

"Ah, fuck. Okay, on it. I'll let Cavallo know too, he's making rounds."

"Okay thanks, I'm going to let the others know."

Fuck, this definitely isn't good. The Crimson Royals ambushed one of our bars and killed six of our men. One of those men was Amante's papà. We retaliated and my papà made a deal with the new president. But seeing those women in their property cuts...fuck. This means their men are in town too. Club women don't go places wearing their cuts without their men. And this also means our agreement has been broken.

Francesco: Hey Papà, there's women here at Luminescence wearing property cuts for Crimson Royals

Giacomo: Are you sure?

Francesco: 100% Positive. (I send a picture of one of the cuts) that's the former president's old lady, if I remember correctly

Giacomo: Shit. How long till the night is over?

Francesco: Still have about two hours. I made sure everyone knows we're on highest alert. I just wanted to give you a heads up

Giacomo: I'm coming down there. Get Amante, Ombra and Fantasma to bring the girls home now

Francesco: Okay, Papà. See you soon

I walk over to where Maeve, my sisters and their friends are.

"I need all of you to head home now," I say to all three of them and their group of friends.

"Why?" Luciana frowns.

Because my sisters are on our MC council, I can't really order them to go home. But this order came from our papà, he's our president. His rules.

"Papà wants you all home. I just saw some women in here wearing property cuts for Crimson Royals. I can't see who they specifically belong to, but they shouldn't be in Illinois at all."

"Holy shit, are you serious?" she asks. "How the fuck did I miss that? And we're council members, you can't make us leave."

"Please, I know you don't want to, but Papà's on his way and asked that you head home."

"Fuck, fine," she says muttering other things that make me chuckle and shake my head.

"Please stay in the big house with my mam and sisters. I'll be home as soon as we close up the club," I say to Maeve.

"What's going on? Who are the Crimson Royals?" she asks.

"Luciana will explain it when you get home," I say as I look at Luciana. She nods back at me. "I love you, Maeve."

"I love you, too," she says as she leaves with my sisters to grab her things.

"If things go down with those assholes, I need to be here," Amante says.

"I know you do. Just make sure the girls are at home and safe. Then have Ombra, Fantasma and a prospect stay with them. And I want three prospects on the main gate tonight. Thomas is there watching the security feeds."

Amante nods at me. "Got it. I'll be back. Those fuckers better not start something again. There's no way they would know we own this club."

"I know, but we can't take any chances. Get them home. And they could know if they've been watching us. We've been slacking with keeping tabs on them."

When the Crimson Royals ambushed us before, we were unprepared. Those cowards attacked our men when they were out having a good time. They threw Molotov cocktails and pipe bombs into the bar. We retaliated by cutting off their pipeline for guns and drugs. And we made sure their council got caught with lots of contraband. They were supposed to be in jail still, but I think it's time to check up on them again. They won't catch us unaware ever again.

"Are they still here?" I hear my papà say from behind me.

"Yup, I've been keeping an eye on them, they're in a group right over there," I say to him. "They seem to be here for the show, no problems from them at all. But I know they had to have seen our cuts. So I'm not sure if we're going to have problems at closing time. And

Amante's coming back after he makes sure everyone's on alert back home."

My papà nods at me. "I figured he'd want to be here."

"I know he wanted to stay, but Luciana comes first."

"I want to know why they're here. We made a deal with that fucking club–Illinois is off limits," my papà growls.

"Could it be just their old ladies that are here? I mean, I don't know why they would be, but maybe?" Cavallo asks.

"No fucking way. We would never let our women go to a state where we're not wanted. Especially alone. I don't see any bodyguards with them. Something's going on," my papà says.

"Why now? Why would they come back now to start shit? Aren't they supposed to stay out of our fucking territory?" Granchio chimes in.

"Just be on alert. I don't like this, and with all these innocent people around, it could get bad really fast."

Chapter Twenty

Giacomo

Nine years ago, when the Crimson Royals MC attacked my club, we made sure their council and a good portion of their members went to prison. In the days after the bombing, we made a deal with the new council—they would stay out of Illinois and we would have no more problems. Which is why I don't understand why their women are here and in our club.

When their council members went to prison, it felt like the new council was satisfied with our deal. I did worry because the son of the old president took over, but I had to give him the benefit of the doubt and work with him. This is on me, though, because I never bothered to check up on them and make sure everything was still in order. That our agreement was still going to be upheld.

At least this time they don't have the element of surprise. On my way here, I stopped at the Hawks Nest. I worry about it because they attacked us here before, so I want to make sure everything is okay there. And that none of the Crimson Royals were there. Our bartender Charlie said it was a normal night, and I made sure to leave a couple of prospects there for extra security. So where the fuck are the men? There's no fucking way they'd let their women come here alone.

Looking at my watch, I see that we still have a little over an hour before we can close up. The atmosphere is getting to be claustrophobic.

It's finally time for last call, and we start to herd everyone towards the exit doors. This is usually the worst time of the night because they don't want to leave. And the people that order at last call are slamming those drinks down. Not a good combo.

"Let's get everyone out of here and close up. I don't like this," I say to my brothers. "And no one goes anywhere alone, everyone in pairs."

Getting everyone out is taking a bit, drunk and moving fast do not go together at all. But at least it's starting to thin out. That's when I hear a woman yelling.

"You're going to pay for what you're doing to my daughter!"

"What are you talking about?" I hear Franco say.

I run into the main area and see Franco with his hands in the air and a group of women wearing Crimson Royals property cuts. One of them is pointing a gun at him.

"Don't act like you don't know who I'm talking about!" she shrieks.

The other patrons are screaming and some are sobbing as my guys try to get them out.

"NO! Everyone fucking stays! You all need to know what he's doing to my daughter!" She's waving the gun around which is making people scream more.

My club brothers are trying to circle her without spooking her, but it's hard because she's smart enough to keep a wall behind her so no one can come up behind her.

"You need to tell me what you're talking about. Please," Franco pleads to her. I can hear the slight tremor in his voice so I know he's not lying, and the look on his face is one of confusion.

"WHY ARE YOU ACTING LIKE YOU DON'T KNOW?" she screams at him again.

I step closer and try to get her attention away from Franco.

"Hey, why don't you give me the gun and we can discuss this. You can tell me who your daughter is and what you think Francesco did to her," I say as calmly as I can.

"Fuck you. You think I'm stupid enough to hand over my gun? You're just as bad as him. I know who you are, Giacomo 'Forza' Bastianini."

Well, shit. The way she sneers as she spits my name out, this has to be some club issue. But what?

"Who are you? And who is your daughter?" I ask her.

"I'm Sonia and my daughter is Tabitha. Your son is fucking treating her like shit, and now she's talking about killing herself because she's in love with him. He's been stringing her along, telling her he loves her and how they're going to get married. Then all of a sudden, he dropped her when he came back from that trip to Ireland."

Holy shit. Tabitha has them all convinced she was in a fucking relationship with my son. And they even knew about our trip. Now we have her mother, her unstable-as-shit mother, waving a gun in our club. And on top of that, she's part of a club we've had problems with before. My gut is saying this isn't going to end well.

"I don't know what you've been told by Tabitha. But we were never in a relationship. I don't even know her," Franco says to her.

"Stop fucking lying!" she screams, waving the gun closer to his face.

Francesco

Holy fuck, what the hell is going on? It's like I'm in a fucking twilight zone version of my life. This woman who says she's psycho Tabitha's mom, is just as crazy as Tabitha.

"Men like you think the you can treat women any way you fucking want. Well, now you're going to pay for treating my Tabitha the way you did. She said you met some Irish bitch and dropped her when you got back, like she was nothing to you."

"Men like me?" I ask calmly. How did we get from one night to a full-blown relationship? How could her mother even believe her story? If we were in a relationship, wouldn't we have met before?

"Yes. Men. Like. You. Club men. You all think women are only good for fucking. The only time you show any respect is when you pick one to be your old lady. And even then, most of you treat them like dog shit stuck to your shoe."

"I'm sorry you think I'm like that. Not all club men are the same. Maybe that's how yours are, but all my club brothers have the utmost respect for women. *All* women."

I need to keep her busy. I have no doubt someone has already called Sal, and I hope he gets here before this woman completely snaps.

She lets out a booming laugh as she cocks the gun.

"There's got to be a way for us to talk this out," my papà says. He's trying to step between me and the gun she's waving.

"Back the fuck up!" she screams at him. "Talk what out? Your son hurt my daughter, and now it's time for your son to hurt."

"Ma'am? I'm going to ask you to put the gun down," Salvatore says. Mac is standing beside him, and both have their guns pointed at her.

"Fuck you, oinker. I know you're part of these assholes."

"What are you talking about?" he asks.

"You're a fucking Mancini. Everyone knows the Mancinis and Bastianinis are in bed together and corrupt as shit."

Whoa. We're not corrupt.

"Ma'am, I'm a Chicago police officer, and I'm going to ask you one more time to put the gun down."

She's laughing like a hysterical hyena. We need to figure out how to get the gun away from her or someone is going to get shot. Probably me, and I don't like that option.

"I'm sorry about Tabitha. I never meant to hurt her."

"Those are just words. Empty fucking words because you don't want to pay for what you did."

"They're not just words, I am truly sorry if I hurt her."

She stops laughing and stares at me. "Liar," she says calmly as she pulls the trigger.

Then I feel a burning sensation in my chest...

Giacomo

The second she pulls the trigger, my men are on her. I watch the scene like it's in slow motion. Patrons screaming, blood flying, and my boy. My son. He falls to the ground, and I rush over to him, putting pressure on his chest. I can hear Mac calling it in.

"I need an ambulance at Luminescence. One down, officers on site. He was shot in the chest. Yes, he's breathing."

"EMTs are coming," Salvatore says to me. "Keep pressure on the wound. I need to get that woman in cuffs."

"Open your eyes, son," I whisper to Franco. He slowly opens his eyes and looks at me. "That's it. Keep them on me."

"Maeve...Saoirse..." he says softly.

"They're fine. You're going to be fine too." I can see the blood starting to seep through my fingers, and his chest struggling to rise and fall. Now I'm not a perfect man, far from it. But I can't go through this again. First my Luciana and now my Francesco. This year hasn't been the best for us as a family. But I can't—no, I won't lose any of my children. I say a silent prayer for someone to please help my Franco.

"Calm Giustizia down. He's not doing any good

yelling at everyone," I say to Amante. He nods and goes over to my other son. Somehow he manages to get him to stop yelling. And keep him from rushing over to where Sal and Mac are cuffing Sonia.

I keep speaking to Franco until I hear the EMTs arrive. I see Schuyler Mancini, wife of Sebastiano, running in with her crew.

"What happened?" she asks as she gently takes my hands off Franco's chest to look at his wound.

"Club trouble and they were targeting Franco. One of the women had a gun she was waving around, then she shot him."

"Okay. We got him. We'll take him to Chicago Memorial. You can follow us there," Schuyler says.

"We'll be right behind you," I respond.

I watch them wheel Franco out.

"I got this here. You and Giustizia go with Franco," Granchio says. "Amante, you drive them. Cavallo, get to the house and pick up the women. They shouldn't be driving."

Amante takes the keys from him and pushes Giustizia and me out the door.

"We'll meet you there after we get this one booked. It looks like a few of them want to join her, they attacked us after she fired."

I don't know how I missed that.

"Thanks," I call out as we run out the door.

"Fuck. I have to call Caitríona," I say, taking a deep breath.

"What's wrong?" Caitríona answers.

"Baby, I need you to stay calm."

"That's never a good thing to say, Giacomo. What's happened?"

"Franco was shot, he's on his way to Chicago Memorial. Cavallo is on his way to you now. Have Fantasma and Ombra stay with Saoirse. She doesn't need to see this."

"What do you mean, 'shot'? Is he alive?"

I can hear her sobbing and the girls in the background.

"He's alive. I don't know how bad it is, but Schuyler came to get him. Sal is still at the club dealing with the shooter."

"Cavallo is here." She sniffles.

"Let me talk to him."

"Okay. Are you at the hospital now?"

"We're five minutes out. I'll be there when you get there. Now put Cavallo on."

"Hey, Forza," Cavallo answers.

"I need you and Azrael to bring the girls to the hospital. Fantasma and Ombra stay with Saoirse. Raziel is on gate duty. No one gets in except patched members. No prospects allowed tonight unless they're family, Mancinis, or Southside."

"Got it, Forza, we'll be there ASAP. Here's Forte."

"Amore. We're heading into the hospital now. Be safe please, and I'll see you soon."

"Please don't let him die. I can't lose any of my babies."

"He's going to be okay, he has a lot to live for and he knows it. I love you."

"I love you too."

I hang up and run inside the emergency doors with my son and brothers behind me.

"My son was brought in. Francesco Bastianini," I try to stay calm while talking to the nurse.

"Giacomo, you can come with me, we just handed Franco off to the surgical team. They're taking him to surgery now," Schuyler says as she leads us to the waiting area.

"How is he? Is he going to be okay?" I ask.

"His pressure dropped in the ambulance, and I'll be honest when I say he's not out of danger yet. But he's in good hands. I know the surgeon that took him in."

"Thank you for helping us. Everything happened so damn fast."

"Giacomo!" I hear my wife calling out. I run over to her and hold her. Then I turn and hug my daughters, Maeve, and the rest of the guys.

"He's been taken to surgery. That's all I know right now."

They all turn to look at Schuyler.

"He's alive. He was shot in the right side of his chest which partially collapsed his lung. But he's still breathing on his own, and he has one of the best surgeons working on him."

All four women hug her and thank her for being here.

"I have to finish up my paperwork and get back to the station. But my shift ends in an hour. I'd like to come back, if that's okay."

"Of course it's okay," Caitríona says to her.

After Schuyler and her partner leave, Salvatore walks into the waiting area.

"How is he?" Salvatore asks.

"We don't know anything yet. He's in surgery." I tell him what Schuyler told us.

"What's going on with that bitch that shot my brother?" Luciana asks Salvatore.

"There were five of them at the show. All five were arrested on gun charges. They each had a gun on them, and Sonia, the one that shot Franco, has the added charge of attempted murder. She won't be getting out anytime soon. The others, though, they could get out on bail until their trial date. It depends if they have priors or not."

The look on my Luciana's face is one of a war going on inside her. I can tell she wants to say more, but it's not Salvatore's fault, so she's holding back.

"I'm off duty now and ready to do my prospect duties," Sal says as he looks at me.

I nod at him while I hold my wife. "Just help keep an eye on everyone and an eye out for anyone wearing Crimson Royals cuts. We don't know where the men are. But they have to be here somewhere."

"On it," Sal replies as he turns to stand by Cavallo.

Four hours later, we're still waiting for news on my boy. Two hours ago, a nurse came out to let us know that the bullet got lodged in his right lung. They got it out and were repairing the damage. He should be out soon, but waiting is the fucking worst. The nurse said as soon as the surgery is over, the doctor will be out to talk to us.

We finally see a doctor-like person coming into the waiting room.

"Bastianini family?" he asks, looking around.

We all stand up at the same time, and it makes him take a step back. I guess as a whole, we can be scary looking.

"How is my son?" Caitríona asks as she steps forward.

"He's going to be fine. The bullet didn't do too much damage. He's in recovery now, and we'll move him to a room within the hour. He's going to need rest for his lung to heal, but he should make a full recovery. I was told this was a targeted shooting?"

"It was. I'm a detective and I've made arrangements to have officers here to stand watch outside his room, so we need him to be in a single room," Salvatore says.

"Not a problem. A nurse will be out to get you when he's settled. I'm here all night and I'll be checking in on him."

"Thank you so much, Doc," I say, shaking his hand. Every one of our group takes their turns thanking him and shaking his hand too.

I wrap my arms around my wife, son, and daughters. Now that we know Franco is going to be okay, we need to find out what is going on with the Crimson Royals.

Chapter Twenty-One

Maeve

Tonight, one of my worst fears came true, I almost lost the love of my life. When I heard Caitríona talking to Giacomo, I knew something was wrong. I felt it even before he called. Sitting in the car on the way to the hospital, I couldn't breathe. What if we get there and he's gone? I can't lose him—I just got him back. Life wouldn't be that cruel to us, right? Our baby girl can't get up and find out her da is gone.

I can hear both Luciana and Isabella sniffling in the car. I look over at Caitríona, and she puts her arm around me.

"My Franco would never stop fighting. Especially now that he has you and Saoirse—there's more for him to fight for," she says softly to me.

"I can't lose him, it took us so long to find each other again. What if I don't get to tell him how much he means to me?" I can't hold back my tears.

"You won't lose him ,Maeve. But you need to be strong for him too," she says.

She's right. I can't break down and fall apart. I have to be strong so that he's strong. Together we're strong. He's going to make it. He has to make it.

When we get to the hospital, we head straight to the surgical waiting area. I look around at everyone, and we all have the same looks on our faces. Worry and fear. When the nurse finally comes out, the news she brings is somewhat comforting. But when the doctor finally comes out, he gives us the best news. My heart felt like it started beating again.

All the guys start talking quietly about the other club and how they must be behind all of this. While we sit and wait for Franco to come out of the recovery room, they finally tell us what happened. My stomach drops when I hear that the woman who shot Franco is psycho Tabitha's mam.

"Do we really think that it's a coincidence that

Tabitha has been terrorizing Franco and now all of us, only to find out that she's a part of the Crimson Royals?" Luciana asks.

"I never saw her wearing a cut or anything that said Crimson Royals," Celestino says.

"Well, she wouldn't, would she? Unless she's a part of the club," Luciana says.

"Even if she wasn't part of the club, she's the old prez's kid. Her brother is the president now, I would think she would at least wear their colors or something to identify who she's with." Isabella frowns.

"Not if her goal was to try and get to our family."

Listening to them talk is making me feel sicker. Was this really just an elaborate set up to get back at the Cimaruta MC? Who does that? I mean, I know they have bad history between the clubs. But this is way over the top. They attacked our club and paid the price, now they want to start something again? What does that do for them?

"We need to figure this out. But first our focus is on getting Franco healthy and back home." Caitríona says to everyone.

"The rules aren't changing. No one goes anywhere alone. Pairs or more, I'm not asking. If I see any of you going somewhere alone? I'll make sure you're stuck at the clubhouse.

Now to get Franco healed and back home where I can show him how much he means to me.

Giacomo

After seeing that Franco is okay with my own eyes, I'm relieved. He's alive. Now it's time to find out what the fuck is going on in my city. And why this psycho family is out to hurt my son.

"I don't want to leave, amore, but I have to. I need to figure out what this night was about. It doesn't feel like it was only about Tabitha lying. Her brother is president and we put their father in prison. I think another war is coming, and we need to be prepared."

"I know you need to go. But with Franco out, you don't have a full council to make decisions."

"Right now I just need the patched members together so I can tell them what's going on. They need to know that they could all be targets. I'm going to leave Cavallo, Azrael, Amante, and Sal here with all of you. I'll take Granchio with me back to the clubhouse. I'll check on Saoirse while I'm there too."

"There's a guard posted right outside the door too. They'll switch out every six hours. And if they need a break for any reason, they'll let you know before they walk away," Sal says to everyone.

"Thank you for everything," Caitríona says to Sal as she hugs him.

"You're welcome, Caitríona, your family and the Cimaruta are our family. Especially now that we're all prospecting. There's nothing we won't do to help you."

"I hope you know that goes both ways," I chime in. "I do need the rest of the prospects at the clubhouse later today. I want all of you to be on the same page with us. And I need more security, so I'll be assigning everyone tasks."

"I'll send a text to everyone and tell them to meet at the clubhouse around noon?" he says as I nod at him. "Now we need Franco to wake up and get better. Because we're going to nail those assholes."

I chuckle at Sal. Listening to the way he talks, you'd never know he was a Chicago Police officer. He sounds like a gangster, which in his defense is what he grew up as. And now he'll be a cop, gangster, and MC member. I hug my girls and then kiss Franco's forehead.

"We need you to wake up and get better," I whisper to him. "Call me if there's any updates or if anything happens."

"I will, amore. Please be safe," Caitríona says.

"Our club will be stronger once all of you become patched members," I say to Sal before I leave.

"The club's growing fast." He chuckles.

"Growing in the right way. Family is what makes our clubs better."

"I agree." He smiles.

"Thanks again for tonight. Now to figure out what the hell is going on."

"I know you don't usually allow prospects at church. But since it's part of a police investigation, maybe you can tell me the history between the Crimson Royals and the Cimaruta?"

"Yeah, it's not really a secret anymore, and I'm sure you'll find files on what happened nine years ago. I'll fill you in on the everything tomorrow at church."

First thing I do is to check on Saoirse.

"How is the princess?" I ask Fantasma.

"She hasn't gotten up at all. How is Bestia? Is he awake? What do we know?" He starts peppering me with questions.

"Bestia is okay, out of surgery but not awake. And we don't know anything. The only thing we know is that the woman that shot him is Tabitha's mother and the wife of the old president of the Crimson Royals."

"Fuck me. Are you serious? I thought this shit was over with them?"

"Yeah, so did I. But I failed the club by not making sure the deal was still in place. And now we know that Tabitha is Grinder's sister and one of our hanger-ons is his brother, Malcolm."

"Tabitha? That crazy psycho that's after Bestia? And that weasel Malcolm? I thought we were releasing him?"

"That's the one. Every patched member is on

their way here. I'm holding church but just to inform all members what's going on. I'm also having all the new prospects in tomorrow for a special church session. I want all of them to know the history between us and the Crimson Royals. And we need a schedule that will work for them to help with security."

Fantasma nods at me. "Should we start doing more checks on the prospects?"

When someone comes to us to prospect, we have them hang around for a few months before giving them an okay. Then it can take up to a year for us to bring them in to be a patched member, sometimes more if we don't see what we want in them. There are always exceptions, like with the O'Callaghan's, Mancini's, and the Southside guys. Their prospect time will be different from others because we already know and trust them.

But there are four guys hanging around right now. We don't usually vet prospects until they're officially given the okay to officially be a prospect. But I think I'm going to have Sebastiano or Salvatore do some digging on them now that this is happening. Usually Franco would take care of this for us...

"Hey Giacomo! I heard what happened to Franco, is he okay?" Sebastiano answers.

"He's going to be okay, thanks. I was calling

to see if you might be able to help me with something."

"Of course. What can I do?"

"We have four new guys wanting to prospect. But I'm not sure I trust them, and now with what happened to Franco tonight, I want to check them out first. I also need info on another person. He's the president of the Crimson Royals."

"Give me their names and I'll see what I can find out."

I give him all five names.

"My parents already consider all of you family, so don't you worry about that. Also papà wanted me to tell you that when it comes time to take care of this situation with Franco, we're there with you. All of us, even the Southside boys that aren't prospecting will be there."

"Grazie. Sal was supposed to let all of you know about the special church tomorrow. I

want to make sure all of you know what's going on."

"We'll all be there. And I'll get these four checked out ASAP."

"I'm sorry for waking you, I did see Schuyler earlier. She left after we knew Franco was going to be okay. I had Cavallo follow her home just in case."

"She's here with me, thank you for the escort. I worry about her when she's on duty."

"I understand. If you ever need extra help you, let us know. Just because you're prospects doesn't mean you don't need extra help too. I know Schuyler has Nico but you can never be too safe."

"That's the truth. I'll see you tomorrow."

"Sounds good. Thanks again."

While I was on the phone with Sebastiano, every patched member of the Cimaruta has shown up. I've forgotten how loud this many men and women can be in an enclosed area.

"Make sure it's not too loud for Saoirse. Then I'll get started," I tell Fantasma. He heads upstairs to Saoirse's room to check on her. He reports back that our princess is sound asleep, and I can't help but smile. She's been the bright spot in all our lives.

"First of all, I want to thank every one of you for getting up so early to show up. Last night at Luminescence, Bestia was shot."

Every member gasps and starts to talk at once. I put my hand up to get them to stop.

"He's going to be okay. He was shot in the chest, but they fixed him and he's in recovery. There's more. The woman that shot him is the mother of Tabitha, the woman who's been stalking him. And she's also the wife of the old president of the Crimson Royals."

"No fucking way," Cupcake says.

"This is on me because I didn't keep tabs on them. And now we know that the new president is not only the old president's son, he's Tabitha's older brother."

"The same club that attacked us nine years ago?" Digger asks.

"Yes," I confirm. "And I think we have a mole. I think it's one of the prospects in waiting."

"This is insane," Cupcake mutters.

"I wanted you all to know this so that you'll be on the lookout wherever you go. No one goes places alone. Always have a partner, and if you feel like you're in danger? Call more help in. No one takes chances."

Everyone stays to talk for a couple of hours. I'm worried that we're going to lose more members before this is over. When I hear back from Sebastiano with the info I need, then it'll be time to contact Grinder and find out what he wants. I'm guessing he wants revenge for his father? But why now? His dad is up for parole soon, whether he gets it is another story. Fuck, I've really dropped the ball on this one.

Chapter Twenty-Two

Francesco

I can hear voices, but my mouth feels like it's glued together. Must. Open. My. Eyes. Since my eyes don't want to listen, I squeeze whatever is in my hand.

"Franco? Baby?" I hear Maeve's sweet voice. "Please open those gorgeous eyes for me."

My gluey eyes finally listen and start to open, and I see my beautiful Maeve.

"Here, son, try and take a sip of this water. Doctor said you might have a really dry mouth.

I look over at my mam and roll my eyes. She puts the straw into my mouth, and I suck a little water. It's like the sweet nectar of life. I stick my tongue out and try to wet my lips a little.

"It's like watching a lizard trying to eat something," my baby sister comments.

"Shush. You be nice to your brother," our mam says.

"That *was* nice." She giggles.

Leave it to Luciana to help make things lighter. I wince as I try to move.

"Don't move too much, baby. Doctor said you'll be really sore for a few days. But they're going to make you get up and walk around today," my mam says.

"Well, that sounds fun," I say hoarsely. "Was anyone else hurt?"

"No, no one else was hurt," my papà says, coming into the room.

"That's good. I still don't understand why this happened."

"What do you remember?" my papà asks.

"I remember bits and pieces. Like she was screaming about her daughter. Who's her daughter? And I saw her and a few other women wearing Property of Crimson Royals cuts."

He nods. "According to the woman that shot you, she's the old lady of the old Crimson Royals' president and the mother of the current president...and Tabitha."

"Crazy psycho Tabitha? What the fuck?"

"If you remember, when the original council and some of the members went to prison, the president's son was voted in to take his place. His name is Marc Binder, road name Grinder. He's the one I made the agreement with. He made it seem like it was all okay.

And it very well could be, but I need to talk to him. This is his mother, so I don't know if he's doing this or she's doing this on her own."

"This is crazy." I frown. "Did she shoot me? And if she did, why?"

"She did shoot you. Tabitha told her that you were in a relationship and that when you came back from Ireland, you dumped her," my papà explains.

"How did she know about Ireland? Tabitha, I mean."

"I think one of the hang-ons is a mole."

"What the fuck? Now we have to worry about the ones wanting to join us?" I grumble.

"Looks like it, from now on we're doing checks before they can even hang around. How are you feeling?"

"Sore. And it's hard to take a deep breath. And this tubey thing is annoying." I complain, picking at a tube that's connected to my side.

"Stop touching the tubey thing," Luciana says, smacking my hand.

"Ouch. Why are you hitting me? Did you see that, mam?"

Luciana rolls her eyes at me while our mam laughs.

"At least I know you're feeling better," our mam says to me.

"It's gonna take more than a crazy lady's bullet to take me out," I say, grabbing a hold of my Maeve's hand. She's shaking as I pull her to me. "I'm okay."

"I thought I was going to lose you," she whispers to me.

"Never, piccola lontra. Death himself is going to have a fight on his hands if he tries to take me."

I move over slowly and pull her to lie on my good side.

"I don't want to hurt you," she says, trying to fight me.

"You're not going to hurt me. Well, you will if you keep fighting me."

She sighs and lies down with me.

"I think that's our cue to leave," Isabella says.

"We'll be back later. There's a police guard outside, and I'm leaving Fantasma with you two," my papà says. "Granchio is with Saoirse."

"Okay, papà, thank you."

"Don't worry about Saoirse, you take care of the whiner here. We got the princess," Luciana says to Maeve.

Maeve smiles at Luciana. "Thank you. Tell her I love her."

"*We* love her." I sigh dramatically.

Maeve giggles. "Yes. We love her."

"See? Whiner. I'll tell her." She carefully gives me a hug. "I'm really glad you're okay. I don't want to know what life would be like without you in it. I love you," Luciana whispers to me.

"You can't get rid of me that easily. I love you, too."

Everyone comes and gives me a hug. I wasn't kidding when I told Maeve the reaper would have a fight on his bony hands if he tries to take me from my family.

Maeve

After everyone leaves, I lay my head on Franco's chest.

"I love you so much, Franco. And I was so scared."

"I'm sorry I scared you, that's the last thing I ever want to do to you."

"It's not your fault. None of this is your fault," she says softly.

"This shit with Tabitha is my fault."

"No, not even that is your fault, I believe she drugged you, and that's all on her."

I love Maeve so much, even though I still feel like part of that situation is my fault. She loves me enough to forgive me for that part I feel is because of me. And she's focusing on the part that isn't my fault.

"I never thought it would get this far, this is fucking crazy. And the fact that she's connected to the Crimson Royals. That's even more screwed up."

"What's the history with that club?" she asks.

"Nine years ago, they attacked us at the Hawk's Nest. They killed six of our men that night, and Amante's papà was one of the ones we lost. We retaliated and helped put their whole council in prison for trafficking. drugs, and gun possession. They all got twenty-five years with the possibility of parole. Then we made a deal with the new president that they would stay out of Illinois. But from what my papà is saying now, we don't know if it's Grinder, the president, calling for this or his mom going rogue."

"Wow. Poor Amante. This situation must be very hard for him."

"It is. I know It's bringing up all kinds of shit for him. That's why Rónán hasn't left Luciana's side. To help out in case something happens. Because we all know that Amante is a little distracted and no one can blame him for that."

I nod as I listen.

"What do you think is going to happen? Will they come after you again?"

"I wish I could say no, but I don't know what they're going to do now."

"Be honest. Do I need to worry about Saoirse?"

"No. Granchio won't let anything happen to her. But maybe we should keep her home till this is over," he says, looking at me. I can see that there's uncertainty in his eyes.

"Okay, I'll call her school and tell them she's going to be out for a while. It's good that she's only in preschool. This would be so much harder if she was in higher grades."

"It would be, this is why my parents suggested homeschooling too. She will learn everything she needs to and there's no shortage of playmates for her."

I know he's right, and with the lifestyle we have, it makes sense to home school.

"I think you're right, we should consider homeschooling."

The smile on my Franco's face tells me I made the right decision.

"Thank you, amore, this means a lot to me."

I snuggle carefully with Franco. At least with Saoirse staying on the property, we can breathe a little easier. Now all I have to worry about is Franco. Because I know that as soon as he's released from the hospital, he's going to go back to his normal routine.

"We'll find a way through this. Before you came back into my life, I had forgotten what it was like to be a part of the Bastianini family. Last night reminded me how good it feels to be with all of you again. How everyone comes together and supports each other. Your mam was hurting and yet she was comforting me. I hope that I can become even half the woman she is."

He smiles at me. "You'll never have to know what it's like not to be a Bastianini. You are a part of us and that will never change. You're here with us forever. You and Saoirse."

We've talked about getting married. Right now it's all about timing. I need this situation with Tabitha to be over and done before I can look to our future. But as soon as all of this is over, we will be husband and wife.

Chapter
Twenty-Three

Francesco

It's been about a month since I was shot, andI'm not completely healed. I get winded faster than before, but even that's getting better. Maeve has been by my side through all of it.

Saoirse is now being homeschooled, granted she's only in preschool, but this will continue even when she's in regular school. We have all decided to teach her the areas we're strong in. So she has lots of teachers teaching her. Cavallo met his woman. Her name is Lila, and she has a five-year-old daughter named Maddie. Saoirse and Maddie have become best friends. There are also other members that have children, and they come over to play with the girls every day.

We finally have all the information we need about

the Crimson Royals. Tabitha was sent to spy on our club. She was sent by Grinder, but we're not sure why. We had an agreement in place. But instead of spying on us, she fixated on me and started stalking me. We know who the mole is, and my papà was right. He's one of the guys waiting to get the okay for him to prospect for us. He's another brother of Tabitha's, and he gave us a fake name when he came to us. We haven't kicked him yet or let him know that we know. We need to keep the element of surprise in order for our plan to work.

Tabitha is still stalking me, she's even started screaming at me in public. It hasn't been easy, but we're making it work. The one thing that I'm most thankful for is that when this happens, Saoirse isn't with me. That's the last thing I need my daughter to see.

Having Callum here has been easier than I thought it would be. He's asked if he can prospect with us, and of course we said yes. He's a really good man, and we're lucky to have him here.

"You can't stop Dolce and me from helping with the Crimson Royals." My sister is yelling at our papà.

"I'm your father and the president of the club. I can make whatever decision I want," he calmly replies.

"Then why did you put us on the fucking council?" she snaps back. Everyone in the room starts to back up from them. No one talks to our papà like that. Not even us.

"Don't you ever speak to me that way, Luciana. I don't give a fuck how old you are, I'm still the head of this family."

"Then stop treating us like we aren't equal to the other council members."

The dilemma right now is that my sister is right. We're all on the Cimaruta council, and for my papà to say that they can't join us on the plan is wrong. But then on the other hand, my papà is more protective because they're his daughters. Sexist? Yeah. but that's the way it is, and you'll never convince my papà to be any different.

"Fine. I won't stop either of you from being there. But you won't go anywhere alone. That goes for everyone."

Luciana finally nods and sits back down.

"Now we know that the Crimson Royals are here in Chicago again. And this time we know where they're staying. They contacted the head of the Chicago Mafia, Enea Mancini, hoping that he would change his alliance from us to them. After Enea talked with Marc, he contacted me. We decided that it would be good for Grinder to believe that Enea is all for the switch in alliance."

"Is Grinder really that stupid? Does he not read the news about the families working together?" I laugh.

"He really does believe that Enea is going to help him take over Chicago from us." My papà sighs.

"At least we have Enea on our side and we have a plan to take the Crimson Royals out once and for all," Fantasma says.

"Everyone knows the plan, right? There can't be any hesitation when it's going down."

Everyone agrees and says they know the plan.

"We've set it up so that it'll go down in one week at the Hawk's Nest. They think we're having a party for Bestia now that he's healed up. I want everyone prepared for anything and everything that can happen. Enea is almost positive that Grinder believes him. But we could be wrong and they could counter us."

"Are we sure of how many of them are here?" Dolce asks.

"Grinder told Enea that he brought eighty-five percent of his patched members. They want to take all of us out. Their numbers are still less than ours, and I've called in our charter clubs from the closest states. Iolar and Drago are coming in two days with all of them. I know there's a few new patched members that haven't met Iolar and Drago yet. But you will now. Even though I've taken over from them, they're still given all the respect that you would give me. They're the reason we're all here."

Everyone in the room is nodding and saying yes.

"Okay, I think that's everything unless someone needs to bring anything up?" my papà says.

No one speaks up, so my papà bangs his gavel to signify the end of church. We all head out of the room and into the main area of the clubhouse. All the kids are playing or watching television.

"You know, attacking papà like that probably wasn't the smartest thing to do," I whisper to Luciana.

"Yeah, probably not. But he has to start treating us the same. I'm on the council just like you."

"Come on sis, you were kidnapped six months ago. It hasn't been that long, and papà is still dealing with that. We all are."

She takes a deep breath and looks at me; there are tears shining in her eyes. "I do know that, Franco, but this is different. They came after you, they tried to take you from us. I need to be there when they're taken down."

I take my sister in my arms and hug her tight. "I get it, I really do. I still remember everything I felt when you were taken. We're going to take those fuckers down together. Just like we took the Raptors down."

She holds me tight. "They won't know what hit them. Stupid stinky buttheads."

I chuckle.

"Da!" We hear my daughter call out as she runs into my arms.

"Hi, my love, are you having fun?" I ask her.

"Yes! Can we go and see our lontras?" she asks.

"Of course we can. Come on aintín Luciana, let's go see the lontras."

Luciana takes Saoirse from me and kisses her face.

"That tickles, aintín."

Luciana laughs and blows a raspberry on her tummy, making her laugh even more.

"Where's your mam?" Luciana asks Saoirse.

"She went to da Callum's house, to take the cookies we made with nana Caitríona."

"Aww, I want cookies. Where's my cookies?" Luciana says as she tickles Saoirse.

She's laughing so hard she can't really answer her.

"I ate yours."

"Whoa. Your daughter just said she ate my cookies!" Luciana looks at me laughing. "Gimme my cookies!"

"Is in my tummy!" she cries out, laughing more.

"Welllll...you'll have to make me more. Or go take some back from Callum." Luciana laughs.

"Nana!" she yells as she's laughing still. "We have to make more cookies!"

My mam laughs as she watches all of us. I can see how happy she is when we're all safe and together. Even after all she's been through, my mam is so strong. Days like today make me forget all the shit we're going through. I can't wait for it to all be over.

Maeve

I love how Callum has become family to the Bastianini family. And the Cimaruta club, he's even asked if he can start prospecting. I think it's a great idea for him to do that. He always told me that he wanted a big family, and being a part of the Cimaruta gives him an instant brotherhood. He's also talked about joining the guys with dancing. Moira is not amused.

"Hey, Maeve." Callum smiles as he sees me sitting outside his house.

"Hey. Caitríona, Saoirse, and I made cookies, and I wanted to bring you some."

"Where is my Saoirse?" he asks, munching on the cookies.

"She ran off as soon as the cookies were in the oven. You know her." I laugh. "She's at the clubhouse. You want to head over with me?"

"Of course. Let me put these inside first."

He runs inside, and I can hear him grabbing more cookies. When he comes back, he has one stuffed in his mouth and one in each hand.

"You're just as bad as Saoirse." I laugh.

He tries to give me a shocked look, but it's not working with the cookie hanging out of his mouth. It's making me laugh even harder. We head out to meet everyone up at the lake.

"Da Callum!" Saoirse says as she runs to him for a hug.

He scoops her up. "How's my favorite girl?"

"Did you know there was a big fire in Chicago? Me and Maddie learned about it today with Granchio."

"Wow! That's crazy!" he says. "Are you having fun learning?"

"Yes! Learning is fun!"

I never would've thought that Franco would be okay with this situation. But he's really trying. I go over and wrap my arms around him.

"Thank you," I say as I kiss him.

"For what?"

"For keeping your promise. For being okay with Callum and loving me the way you promised."

"You're welcome. I told you that this time was forever. I realized that I said that before, but I was stupid. By the time I realized what I had done, I thought it was too late."

"Never too late." I smile.

Chapter Twenty-Four

Francesco

My grandfathers arrived today with the Galway and Florence Cimaruta clubs. I hate that the reason they're here is because of me. My papà keeps telling me that this would be happening even if this situation with Tabitha didn't happen. I'm not sure I believe him.

Tomorrow is the day we take down the Crimson Royals. Just like T-Rex from the Feral Raptors, Grinder thinks that he can over take our club and territory. It's not something new, there's always other clubs that want to take over our territory. Especially since we're the mother club, we get more threats than our charter clubs. It's not as bad as it was when my grandfathers were presidents, but we have our moments of dealing with shit like this.

Eight years ago, my papà proposed that the clubs stop running drugs and guns. This was before my twin and I became prospects. When the word got out that the Cimaruta was getting out of the business, it seems like it became open season on members. By the time my twin and I started prospecting, things were settling down a little. You would think it would lessen the target on us, but no. It felt like getting out of the illegal stuff put a bigger target on our backs.

We have over one hundred members here for this. Almost all the members in the surrounding states and four chapters from Europe are here for this. The hardest part about all of this is we don't have a guarantee everyone will be alright when all this is over. There's too many of us to fit into our council room so we're in the main room for this. My papà hits his gavel on the counter.

The Mancini and Southside Mafia's are here with us too. Not just the ones that are prospecting with us. This is a family situation and the families have answered to stand with us.

My papà clears his throat and starts church. "First of all, I want to thank everyone for being here. We appreciate all the help you're giving us. Second, I'd like to introduce the head of the Mancini mafia, Enea Mancini and the head of the Southside mafia, Elio Salvadori. Thank you both for being here to help us fight."

Enea and Elio both nod their heads at my papà.

"So the plan is that we'll all head to our club's bar, the Hawk's Nest, at about six. It's being set up right now for the party. That's our ruse, it's a party for Bestia's recovery. Grinder is the current president of the Crimson Royals. He contacted Enea in hopes that he would align with him and his club and help him take our club out. Which as you can see, isn't happening."

Everyone chuckles.

"It is laughable that Marc thinks that all it would take is for him to meet with me to get me to change my alliance. I'm sure you all know the history my family has with Giacomo and his family. So trust in the fact that you won't be watching your backs around us. We've got your backs. I did make Marc believe that I was willing to change my alliance to help him. It was the only way that I could insure we knew what he was planning."

Maybe now we'll find out why Grinder changed his mind about our truce.

"Marc and I made a plan that they are going to ambush all of you at the party. It was the only place I could think of where we could contain them and everything that's going to happen." Enea says.

"What exactly are they planning?" Asks Sandman, president of the Chaotic Warriors MC, one of our chapter clubs out of Indiana.

"Their plan was to place bombs at the bar. But I talked him out of that. I told him something like that would bring a lot of law enforcement out, not just local but federal. That made him sit up and think twice. I told him with guns and fists, I can help him keep it local. But if he does anything else, I'll walk away and let him deal with the fallout. So he agreed. I don't trust him, so I've had one of the Southside boys, Justin, following him since he first contacted me." Enea explains.

"So we're sure there's no bombs being placed anywhere near the Hawk's Nest?" Granchio asks.

"I'm sure. Besides Justin following Marc, I've had others watching the bar 24/7." Elio says.

"Now we all know what the worst case scenario is. Those of you who were with us nine years ago saw what happened then. Only this time they don't have the upper hand. We do." Forza says.

But that doesn't mean there won't be any casualties. That's the thing my papà isn't saying. But we all know what can happen in situations like this. The room is eerily silent as we all soak that in. This time tomorrow, we might not all be here. And that isn't sitting well with me, a lot of that has to do with the fact that this is because of me. Okay fine, not *because* of me, but *for* me. That doesn't make it any better.

"Okay, I know it's a lot to ask but I'm going to ask that no one leaves the property until we go for the party. I don't want any of you in their line of sight for any reason." Forza says. "And when we are at the bar, when it's time, you all need to make sure your women and children are in the rooms we tell you to put them in. That's the only way I can make sure they're all safe."

"Oh and another thing, I made sure that Marc's meeting with me at seven tonight before we head to the Hawk's Nest. I didn't want him or any of his guys to be waiting at the Hawk's nest or to ambush you on the way. And before you ask, yes, I do think he's going to listen to the times I've set to meet me. Because I told him if he wants my help and my family's help, he needs to do this my way. And he *really* wants my help." Enea says.

"Did Grinder say why he's doing this?" I ask Enea.

He nods. "He said that when he made the agreement with Giacomo, he did it to stop the fighting at the time. He didn't want you to come after them right away. But now he's ready and feels that he can avenge his father and club brothers."

I frown while we listen to Enea. We thought that this shit with the Crimson Royals was over and done. All the while that little shit was plotting to come and get us this whole time. And on top of it all? He sent his sister and brother to try and infiltrate us. Tomorrow night, he's going down.

Tonight, we're having an impromptu barbecue. We're trying to keep everyone calm, but I'm not sure how well it's going. The bright spot to all this is having my grandparents here. I miss them and I need them to be safe tomorrow. We tried asking my Nonno Pietro and Granda Liam to stay in the panic rooms with the others and got an earful about how they're not too old to fight with the club. And anyone who even suggests it will see what they can still do.

"Are you doing okay?" my nonno asks me.

"I just want this to be over. I thought that when Maeve and Saoirse moved over here my life would finally be complete. But I've put them in this damn situation, and I can't guarantee that everyone will come out okay."

"Look at me, Franco. None of this is your fault, and I don't want you to ever say that again. This is something that started way before you were a Cimaruta."

"But, nonno—"

"No buts. You need to get your head on straight and realize not even that woman coming after you is your fault. She was sent by the fucking Crimson Royals, and that wasn't because of you. We will never know why they came after us nine years ago. But it wasn't because of you."

I look down at my feet. I get what my nonno is saying, Tabitha could've set her sights on any of us. It just so happened to be me.

CHAPTER TWENTY-FOUR

"Are you listening to me?" Nonno says, breaking into my thoughts.

"Sì, nonno. I'm listening. It's just hard to not feel like the Tabitha thing isn't my fault."

"You just happened to be the one that she focused on. It could've been any of the brothers."

"You need to listen to your nonno," Granda Liam adds in. Great, now I have both of them coming at me.

"There's no way any of us could've seen any of this coming. It was supposed to be over nine years ago. The Crimson Royals chose to open it all up again," Granda Liam says.

I sigh and nod. "I get it. I really do."

"Then stop being a moper and focus on what we all need to do tomorrow night to put an end to all of it."

"Did you just call me a moper?" I look at my Granda. He's smiling at me.

"I did."

I laugh at both of them. Family. It's all I have to count on in this world.

Maeve

Lying in bed, I keep tossing and turning. I can't get my mind to settle down, I'm so worried. Franco's arms wrap around me, and it helps to calm me a little.

I wiggle my ass against him and hear him moan

behind me. He reaches around and slides his hand into my shorts, circling my clit.

"Baby," I moan.

"I need you, Maeve," he growls out as he's pulling my shorts off. I'm trying to help him but my hands, are just getting in the way. He rubs the tip of his cock against my clit.

"I need you in me, please," I beg him.

"Fuck," he moans as he's sliding into me. "You're so fucking wet."

"Fuck me, please." I gasp.

He moves faster as he rubs my clit. Suddenly, he pulls out of me and flips me onto my back. He lifts my legs so they're straight against his chest and rubs his cock along my slit. He's driving me fucking crazy, and he knows it.

"Franco, please." I beg for more.

Franco smiles at me as pushes back into me. "So fucking deep," he whispers.

He pumps into me faster as I gasp.

"Come for me, amore," he rasps out while I watch him lick his finger then circle my clit. I explode around him.

"Ah, fuck yes," he says as he comes with me.

After we catch our breath, he slowly lowers my legs and kisses me. I can still feel him inside me.

"I love you so damn much, Maeve."

"I love you, Franco. Always."

He slowly pulls out of me and goes to the bathroom, coming back with a warm washcloth, and gently cleans me up. Then he takes it back to the bathroom. I realize that this is something he always does for me after we make love. He never leaves me to clean myself, it's always him that does it for me.

We snuggle together and drift off to sleep. Please let everyone be okay tomorrow.

Chapter Twenty-Five

Maeve

I'm so scared about what's going to happen tonight. I know it has to happen but it doesn't make it easier. If things go wrong tonight, I could lose a lot and I'm not sure I can handle that. This family, the club, they all mean more to me than I can explain. Because the ruse is that it's a party for Franco, we're all going to be there. Even Saoirse. This part of the plan makes me nervous, I don't want her to see this side of MC life. But she has to be there in case Grinder has someone watching the bar. We have to keep up the ruse of a normal party. Then, when the time gets closer, she will be protected by Granchio. I know he's just one man, but I have no doubt he will lay his life down for her.

There's a seven rooms in the back of the bar that

are built like a panic rooms. They're bulletproof and only the family knows how to access it. They are disguised as regular rooms, storage areas and even a few rooms with couches for people to sleep off their alcohol if needed. That's where my baby and I will be with Fantasma and Granchio. I know they're not happy about having to miss the fight.

Giacomo wants Caitríona, Isabella and Luciana in there with us too. Isabella and Luciana flat out said no. Caitríona hasn't decided yet. The wives, girlfriends and kids that are here will be in the panic rooms too. Some of the chapter club members brought their families. We had to keep up the look of the party. I know they're all worried and that makes me sad. Because of the situation, most of them didn't want to bring their kids, but again, we had to keep up the appearance of a party.

We have about four hours before we're supposed to head to the bar. The nauseousness in my belly is getting worse and worse.

"Please promise me you won't take unnecessary chances." I beg Franco.

"I promise, piccola lontra, I won't do anything stupid."

"Maybe you can come into the panic room with us." I plead with him.

"You know I can't do that, Maeve. I know you're worried. But I won't leave my club family out there fighting a situation that is my fault."

Nothing we say to Franco has convinced him that this isn't his fault. I wish I knew how to help him to see that. I can't help the tears that are streaming down my face. My greatest fear could come true today and I'm helpless to stop it.

Franco holds me tight. "Please don't cry, Maeve. We're going to be okay. I love you."

"I love you, too." I sniffle. "I'm just so scared that I'm going to lose you. Or we'll lose one of our family."

Franco tilts my chin up so I'm looking into his beautiful face. "I won't lie to you, I'm worried too. But we need to do this."

"I know. This is the side of MC life that I hate. I wish we knew why he chose now to do this."

"He chose to do it now because he thinks we're the most vulnerable. But he's wrong."

I know there's things Franco can't tell me about club business. And I accept that. I just hope that today comes out in our favor.

Francesco

"You can stay here at home. Do you want to stay here?" I ask her.

"No. I need to be there with you. I-I can do this." She sniffles.

I can't handle watching my girl cry. I never could and this time is no different. There's nothing I can really say that will make any of this better.

"I know you can baby, but you don't have to."

"I have to be there. They know who I am and if they're watching and I'm not there, they might try something different. They tried to take you from me. From Saoirse. I need to see them go down."

Maeve stands up straighter. I chuckle softly. That's my fighting Maeve, she's stronger than she thinks. I do hope that tonight goes well for all of us.

We all pile into various cages and set off to the Hawk's Nest. Everyone is wound up so much that you can taste the tension in the air. I can't help but look out the window as we drive to the bar. Tonight feels like the night I got shot. I send a silent pleading to the gods that everyone is alive after tonight.

Everyone tries to relax a little, we have about two hours before Enea is supposed to meet up with Grinder. Enea is with us until he's supposed to meet up with Grinder. The updates from Justin is that Grinder and the guys he brought are all at the hotel they're staying at. Their women are there too. So for once I don't have to worry about Tabitha showing up at the Hawk's Nest.

Maeve

The night I almost my Franco, I swore that I needed to be there when the club got its revenge. I don't know how I can help but I just know I need to be there. The panic rooms we'll be in has the monitors for the security system. Watching the fight is going to be hard. But I need to make sure my family is okay through it. My family. I never thought I would have this family again and now that I do, it's like no time has passed.

I thought that Franco and I were in love before. And I was right. But nothing compares to our love now. Watching him be a da to our daughter, that was something I hoped but didn't think would happen. If you had asked me before, I would've said that Franco won't forgive me for keeping her from him. But now? He's forgiven me completely and embraced us both with no lingering anger. All the anger and hurt that I held on to is gone. I don't have the fear that he's going to leave me anymore. I still don't like the women touching him at the shows, but I understand what Luciana and Isabella have been saying. Our men love us, they're ours and the trust between us is what makes it work. It's more than I wished for.

Chapter Twenty-Six

Enea Mancini

It's almost time for me to go and meet with Marc. We've had our share of battles and heartache in our family. When my son, Sebastiano's wife was kidnapped, the Cimaruta came to help us. So now it's our turn to help them. When I met up with Marc earlier this week, the anger that was coming off him was stifling. He ranted about how the Cimaruta stole his dads life from him by setting him up. How they lied about what the Crimson Royals were doing. That they've never done anything illegal.

That last one made me laugh. I grew up in a mafia family and no matter how much we want to be law abiding citizens, we will always have our toes in the underworld. That is the same for the MC's.

Giacomo and I have been trying to get our families to do better. It's been a long process and it will never be perfect. But our goal is to make Chicago a safer place for our families and the people that live here. Marc is doing the opposite from what we are doing. And he needs to know that he can't just come here and try to change things. I understand he's angry about his father and club brothers. But in truth, they did it to themselves. They attacked the Cimaruta and lost. That was the consequences to the attack, their whole council went away. Plus some of the regular members. It's the price we all pay for the lives we lead.

I go over to Giacomo to let him know I'm going to be leaving.

"I think it's time I head over to the Legacy to meet Marc. I'm going to take Sebastiano, Salvatore and Mario with me."

Giacomo nods at me. "I wish I could send some of my guys with you. This whole situation isn't sitting well with me. I'm going to send Raziel and one of our prospects, Anthony to tail you. You never know what Grinder is going to do."

"Thanks. But technically since my boy and nephew are prospecting with you, I will have some Cimaruta with me."

"True." He chuckles. "Be safe. And we're ready if you need us."

"Be ready for plan B. I don't have high hopes for Marc to follow our agreement."

Giacomo says okay to me as we shake hands. I

didn't say it but tonight makes me worry too. Especially with all the women here. The women in my family are here, but they know that when it's time, they need to be where Giacomo puts his family.

Wars are never pretty.

"Are we sure he's going to show up?" My son, Sebastiano asks.

I nod. "He's so desperate to take over the Cimaruta, he'll be here."

"Is that him? He is little." Mario chuckles.

But to be fair, I think everyone is little next to Mario. The man is six-foot-six and well over three hundred pounds. If I didn't know him, I would probably stay clear of him.

"Well it looks like he's brought his whole club." Salvatore says under his breath.

We see Marc heading inside the hotel with about twenty men. He didn't mention to me that he had this many men with him. He just said a *few*.

"Text Giacomo and give him a heads up on the amount of men that are here. Be discrete." I say to Sal.

Fuck. I need to come up with an alternate plan.

The original plan was for us to go to the Hawk's Nest and take the Cimaruta out. He's going to be a pain in my ass.

"Enea!" Marc calls out as he's heading towards me.

He's loud enough that people are turning to look. I don't like that. So I walk towards him so he'll stop yelling.

"I thought you only had a few of your men with you?" I say as we shake hands.

"At the beginning I did. But when word got out in my club and more showed up today. And I can't deny my club their revenge." He's smirking.

Fucking arrogant prick. He's actually smirking at me.

"You realize that with more men, they'll see us coming right? The idea of this was to be in and out without complications."

"Well more men means we get all of them, right?"

This bastard is still smirking at me and I want to wipe it off his face. He's going to learn really fast that you don't fuck with Enea Mancini.

"Since you can't follow the agreement we made, I think we should just call the whole thing off."

The smirk on his face disappears and he looks panicked.

"Wait. You can't back out."

I laugh. "Sure I can. I don't deal with men who think they can make the rules as they go. We had an agreement as to what would happen tonight. You decided that you knew better and want to change it."

I can see the wheels turning in his head. If he's smart, he'll wise up and change his tone. I turn to walk away.

"Wait! Okay, we'll stick to the original plan. Five of my guys. The rest will go back to the hotel and wait." He says.

I turn back around and hear his men grumbling. He's telling them that they need me to get this done. He has no idea.

"If you change anything or I see any of your guys around, you will be the one that loses. I will walk away and leave you to deal with all of the fallout."

He nods at me, then turns to his men and picks the five he'll take with us. Then tells the rest to go back to the hotel and don't fuck this up for him. These young fucks think they run things. I'm going to like showing him that he isn't who he thinks he is. You don't retaliate against anyone just because you're mad at the consequences of another war. If I ran my family like that? We'd probably all be dead.

We watch his guys leave, he gives then another warning not to leave the hotel until they hear from him. Most of his club is young. And it'll be interesting to see if they listen to him.

"Make sure Giacomo knows the situation and that they have more members here. That they're probably going to pose a problem. Also let him know that I think he should get the women and kids situated right now. I don't trust any of these assholes. And I think Marc has a different plan than what we agreed to. Tell him plan

B is probably going to be in play." I say softly to Sebastian.

My son walks away to call Giacomo. Marc is watching my son and I don't like the look on his face. If he touches any of my boys there will be hell to pay.

"Where is he going? And who's he taking to?" Marc frowns.

"None of your fucking business." I say to him. That gets me a look from him that I know means he's going to start unnecessary shit. Fucking hell. Plan B it is.

Plan B is that Salvatore will let his partner Mac know we might need back up. I'm not worried about them coming for us or the Cimaruta. We've had a truce with the Chicago police that as long as we keep under the radar, they stay out of our business.

"We should probably get going?" Marc asks me.

"Waiting on my driver. He'll be here in a few minutes."

I can see how anxious he's getting. Wait till he sees what's waiting for him at the Hawk's Nest. Everyone stays quiet on the way to the bar, making sure we keep an eye on the Crimson Royals following behind us.

Chapter Twenty-Seven

Francesco

After my papà got a call from Sebastiano, he said we need to get all the women and kids into the back rooms. That's not a good sign. We have seven rooms in the back that all serve a dual purpose of rooms and panic rooms. They seal up into one large area. My papà made one of the rooms a play room with toys and a TV for the kids to be in. Hopefully it makes it easier for them to be in there. At least they won't be able to hear anything back here.

"Don't forget your promise, Franco. I know you can't stay out of the fight. But please. We need you to be okay when all of this is over." Maeve pleads.

"I know, amore. We're all going to be as careful as we can," I reassure her as I hold her tight.

I watch her go over to Callum, I know she's worried for him too. He's holding Moira and she's crying. Luciana and Isabella's friends have never seen this side of club life. They all look scared and I don't blame them.

I crouch down to Saoirse's level, giving her a hug and kiss. "You listen to your nana, mam, and Granchio."

"Okay, da. Is everything okay? Why are we back here?" She asks looking around.

"Nonno Giacomo made these rooms so you and the other kids can play in here. And you'll be safe."

She nods at me. "Okay, da. I promise to listen."

"That's my girl."

I go over and hug my mam. She grabs Celestino and me tightly.

"You both need to be careful. And please try to watch out for your sisters. I hate that they're going to be out there." She whispers to us as she holds us tighter.

"We will, mam." We both say together.

My sisters being out there is worrying me and Celestino. We tried to get them to stay in the panic rooms. But of course they shot us down fast than we could get the words out. The hardest thing I have to do tonight is close these doors on my family. But it's for all of their safety. I couldn't live with myself if something happened to any of them.

While we're waiting, Sebastiano gives me a call.

"Hey Bastian, are you guys on your way?"

"Yeah, we're about fifteen minutes away. My papà says that he doesn't think Grinder's going to follow the plan they made. This is going to be over fast, he hates situations like this. Are the women and kids safe?"

I sigh. "Yeah, they're all in the rooms and the rooms are sealed. Why does your papà think Grinder isn't going to follow the plan?"

"First because he said he had five guys with him. When he showed up, he had almost twenty. He tried to act like he was above my papà. It was fucking hilarious. Grinder actually thought he could tell my papà what to do. He's still pissed."

"He should be. Apparently Grinder doesn't have any respect for others." I say.

He chuckles. "Nope. Okay we're almost there. You guys ready? Sal called Mac and they're waiting close by to be ready after we all get inside."

"Okay we're ready. See you soon."

I hope the plan goes the way we planned it. But after hearing that Grinder is already changing what he agreed to, I'm not so sure.

We're all ready for guns blazing. The hard part is acting like we're not ready for it. Be calm and party like normal. Easy, right?

We finally see headlights parking in our lot. Game. On.

"Okay guys. We know what Grinder wants. Let's make sure he doesn't get it." My papà says to everyone just as the doors open and Enea and his boys walk in first. Some of us turn and look then turn back to our drinks. I can feel my brothers vibrating around me.

The next thing that happens shouldn't have come as a surprise. We knew that asshole Grinder wasn't going to follow the plan.

Bullets start flying past me and Cavallo who is sitting next to me.

"You assholes think that some stupid agreement is going to keep you safe from us?" I hear someone yell from behind me.

I'm turning to face whoever is behind me. Everything is happening so fucking fast. Bullet and fists are flying. During all of this I'm trying to keep track of my family. It's then I notice that there are more people here that I don't recognize. Fuck. I make my way over to my papà.

"There's more Crimson Royals. I counted at least fifteen." I say to him.

"I know. I'm guessing all twenty that Enea saw are here." He says as we see Grinder headed our way.

"You'll pay for sending my dad to prison you corrupt fucks." He screams at us with his gun raised and pointed at my papà. Fuck no. He's not going to kill my papà for putting his shitbag dad in prison. And corrupt? What the fuck does he think his club does?

I raise my gun and aim it at Grinder. I squeeze the trigger and watch the red bloom in his chest like it's in slow motion.

There's bodies littering the floor of the bar, it's a mixture of Cimaruta and Crimson Royals. Only a few of them aren't moving and I don't think any of them are ours. The sirens are getting louder, Mac came through for us.

The cops burst into the bar, guns drawn.

"This is the Chicago police! Drop all your weapons and get down on the ground." Mac says.

"Fuck you, pig!" One of the Crimson Royals yells before firing a shot at the officers. He went down before he could get a second shot off. Luckily he was a shit shot and didn't hit anyone.

And just like that it's over. The adrenaline is still pumping through my body and it's starting to make my body tremble. I look around again and see some of our brothers being taken out to ambulances waiting outside. I see my club and family standing around, bloodied but safe. My nonno and granda are safe, I can see cuts on them. They're standing and talking to Mac. Fuck, they're tougher than most give them credit for.

My sisters have blood on them, I'm guessing some is theirs. I go over to them to check them out, Celestino beats me there and is looking them over.

"Are you okay?" I say as I inspect them.

"Just a bullet graze." Isabella says.

"Knife cuts. Nothing major." Luciana says.

"And you?" I ask my twin.

"Bullet graze and knife cuts. Nothing major either."

Relief floods me as I hear their injuries.

Callum comes over to us.

"Wounds?" I ask him.

"Aye, knife cuts is all. That was fucking intense."

I nod at him. "That went better than the last time they attacked us. At least we were prepared."

"I can't even imagine how this would've gone if they ambushed us." He frowns.

Tonight felt like it went on for hours. When in reality, it was over in thirty minutes. Thirty fucking minutes and several lives were lost because one asshole couldn't deal with his past.

"No Cimaruta, Mancini or Southside were taken from us, but we did have a total of ten wounded. They're all headed to the hospital. Seven of the Crimson Royals were killed and seven more wounded. The rest have been arrested and are headed to jail as we speak." Forza says to everyone left behind.

"I don't think that was the whole Crimson Royals club." Enea says. "The way Marc talked was like there were more members waiting back in California."

"I'll get in touch with the LAPD, let them know what happened out here. Maybe they can round up the rest of them and make sure the ones in prison know that any more retaliation will see them serving their whole sentence." Salvatore says.

"Thank you." Forza says. "Bestia, can you go and open the panic room, please."

I nod at my papà, then head back to the rooms.

As soon as Maeve's eyes land on me, I can see the relief in her face. She runs to me with my mam and I embrace them both.

"Did we lose anyone?" My mam asks.

"No. We have some wounded. But we didn't lose any Cimaruta, Mancini or Southside."

"Thank god. I don't know what I would've done if we lost anyone."

The relief in her voice is loud and clear. She heads out to find my papà and siblings. Some of the women and kids in the rooms are the families of our wounded. My papà will make sure they're taken to the hospital to be with their men.

"I'm so happy you're okay." Maeve says. "Is it really over?"

I don't know how to tell her I'm not sure. Tabitha is still out there and I have a feeling knowing one of her brothers is dead and the other in jail isn't going to sit well with her.

"It is for now, amore. For tonight, everything is okay."

She nods and I holder tighter. I wish I could feel better after what just happened. I'm pretty sure the Crimson Royals are done. But now Tabitha is alone and who knows what she'll do. I just hope she chooses to go back home and start over there. But we still need to find out what happened to George. His family deserves closure and she's the only one who can give that to them.

Epilogue

Francesco

It's been a month since that night at the Hawk's Nest. So far we haven't seen or heard from Tabitha. I still hope that she's gone back to California. And that we won't see or hear from her anymore. The members of the Crimson Royals that made it out alive that night are all in prison back in California. They went on trial here in Illinois, got twenty-five to life. Then they were sent to California to face charges there and got ten to twenty. They're able to serve the sentences concurrently and in California. But they still have to serve a minimum amount of time. Depending on how they are in prison, they could be there for the rest of their lives. At least Grinder has been reunited with his dad.

Grinders mom and the other women are serving a seven to ten year sentence each here in Illinois. We're keeping up on everything they're doing in case they get out early. They asked to be transferred back to California. But the judge denied their requests. He said it worried him to have all of them back in California. Especially knowing that they are the wives of the MC that has been taken down.

The Crimson Royals have been completely disbanded. None of the remaining members wanted to take over. They all agreed to walk away and try and join other clubs. Now whether they'll keep this agreement and stay away from Illinois and any Cimaruta chapter is another story.

Our club family has gone through so much lately. Starting with my baby sister being kidnapped to the shootout at the Hawk's Nest. And then Cavallos's daughter, Maddie, was kidnapped by her bio-papà, Travis. We got her back with minimal damage to our club. Travis' wife, Shawna was killed, but I'm not sure I'm sad about that. We found out after that she had abused and terrorized Maddie the whole day they had her. Travis and Shawna had three boys, Blake, Kyler and Parker. Cavallo and Lila have brought them into our family. I asked them why and Lila said it wasn't the boys fault their parents were assholes. And they're Maddie's half brothers. As always, the whole club has stepped in to help them.

My grandparents are still staying with us. They want to spend time with Maeve and get to know Saoirse. And they wanted to be here for Luciana and Rónán's wedding, which is this weekend.

I've been trying to find the right time to ask Maeve to marry me. Luciana suggested I do it at her wedding since everyone will be there. She told me to use my speech to them to ask Maeve to be my wife. Something I should've done years ago.

Maeve

Luciana and Rónán's wedding was beautiful. Their love shines through everything they do together. We were all a part of the wedding as bridesmaids and groomsmen. Saoirse and Maddie were the flower girls, Blake was an usher, he helped get everyone to their seats then came and stood with all of us. Kyler and Parker were the ring bearers. I don't know how they did it, but they included everyone. Made everyone feel like they were an important part of their day.

Listening to them recite their vows to each other

brought tears to my eyes. The look on Giacomo's face when Raziel announced Rónán and Luciana Bastianini-O'Callaghan. That was priceless.

Celestino's and Isabella's speeches to Rónán and Luciana brought more tears from everyone. Then it's Franco's turn, I love watching him, he carries himself with such masculinity and grace. And he's mine.

"Rónán, good luck with my baby sister. She's been a pain in my ass for as long as I can remember. And now? She's your pain in the ass." Everyone laughs at Franco.

"I don't care. I love her and she can be the biggest pain in the ass to me. She's stuck with me forever." Rónán responds.

Franco laughs more. "We have that on camera. So you can't take it back. On a serious note, I love you, Luciana and I'm so glad you found your forever."

Luciana blows a kiss to Franco and nods her head at him. There's something going on—he turns to face everyone and walks over to me.

"Luciana and Rónán gave me their blessing to use my speech to them for another reason."

He stops in front of me and smiles, dropping to one knee. Oh my god.

"Maeve. I knew when I met you that you were the one for me. We were fourteen years old and I just knew. We spent four beautiful years together. Then I made the worst mistake of my life and let you go. I didn't know it at the time but I left you to take care of our daughter alone. Something I'll never be able to make up to you. Then fate saw fit for us to find out way back to each other and gave me a second chance to be with the love of my life. I promised you that I would make it all up to you. I'll never let you go again, no matter how tough life may get, I'm all in. Will you be my wife?"

My tears are streaming down my face. "Yes." Is all I can get out.

Franco places the most gorgeous claddagh ring on my finger. The ring is a traditional setting except that the heart between the hands is a diamond. It's the most beautiful ring I've ever seen. He leans in and kisses me as the room erupts with cheers.

"I love you, Franco." I say as I hold him.

"You are my everything, Maeve. Thank you for giving me the chance to show you how much you mean to me."

"Thank you for keeping your promise and making all my dreams come true."

About the Author

Hi! I'm Natalie. I published my first book, Aftermath in August 2021. I've been lucky enough to find my own insta-love-at-first-sight person. We have a daughter who drives us crazy and a corgi who adds to the chaos. I love hockey (Chicago Blackhawks), MotoGP (Motorcycle Racing), and baseball (Chicago Cubs). When I'm not writing, you can find me studying or crafting. Or crafting when I should be studying.

Nataliearthurbooks.com

Giovanna

Everything I thought about my life was a lie and because of that, trust became non-existent for me. Then I met Declan. He pushed his way into my life, determined to prove to me that not everyone is a liar. He's a hockey player and we all know the reputation of hockey players. But I want to trust someone again...maybe he's the one?

<u>Declan</u>

Hockey has been my focus for as long as I can remember. The day I met Giovanna, my life changed. Hockey would always be my first love. But she would be my last. Something happened to her and she's afraid to trust me. But that's okay, I'll show her that I'm real. That we're real.

Aftermath is the first book in my Mancini Legacy Series. All books are standalone, but it's best if read in order. There is mention of characters from my Cimaruta MC Chicago Series.

https://books2read.com/Aftermath-ManciniLegacy

Sebastiano

I had given up on meeting my person, content to be the protector of my family. Then one day I met her. But someone else was laying claim to her. If she was happy, I would step back and watch her from afar. But then I saw the marks on her and I knew I needed to save her.

Schuyler

It seems like I've been struggling most of my life. Just my sister and me against the world. Then I thought I met the man of my dreams. Turns out he's the man from my nightmares. I can't run and I can't escape from him. Then I met Sebastiano. He made me feel safe from the moment he took my hand in his. He says I will be his, but he doesn't know about the monster that's in my life. The one that won't let go.

Saving Her is the second book in my Mancini Legacy Series. All books are standalone, but it's best if read in order. There is mention of characters from my Cimaruta MC Chicago Series.

https://books2read.com/SavingHer-ManciniLegacy

<u>Luciana</u>

Women on an MC council? It's unheard of until now. Love at first sight? That's a new one for me too. I was convinced I didn't need someone to make me happy.

Then I slammed into Rónán.

Literally.

In an instant, he turned my world upside down. But can he handle the MC life?

<u>**Rónán**</u>

My life was going the way I planned it. Then the most beautiful woman stepped into my path and changed my life forever. I know she's keeping things from me. And that's okay...for now.

Because she's mine.

She just doesn't know it yet.

Choices is the first book in my Cimaruta MC Chicago Series. All books are standalone, but it's best if read in order. There is mention of characters from my Mancini Legacy Series.

https://books2read.com/Choices-CimarutaMCChicago

Amante

Relationship? No.

Love? Hell no.

Forever? Never.

A quick hook up and that was that. I had my family and my club and that's all I needed. Until the day she walked in. With her I wanted more than one night, but when I got out of the shower she was gone. But I will find her. Then I'll just have to convince her we belong together.

<u>Charmaine</u>

Love is nothing but a lie. I watched my parents crash and burn and nothing and no one could change my mind. Until him. My tattooed, hunky biker man. Wait, did I say mine? That can't happen. But he says all the right things, and makes me feel like I'm the most special girl in the world. Can we make it work?

Notch the Plan is part of the Notchin' Boots Series. There is mention of characters from my Mancini Legacy Series and my Cimaruta MC Chicago Series.

https://books2read.com/NotchThePlan-NotchinBoots

Hollis

The people you're born to don't always turn out to be your 'family'. Families can be chosen, and I chose the Cimaruta MC. They've been there with me for the last six years, and I thought I had everything I needed. One night was all it took to make me want more. But she's hiding something from me and I need to know what it is. I will save her from anything. That much I do know.

Lila

My life was finally going smoothly. It was me and my daughter against the world. I worked at a club called Club Curve—I'm a curvy girl, so why not? Then one night, HE walked in. Now he's turning my life upside down and I'm not sure how to feel about it. My biggest fear is about to become a reality.

Just as you are is a stand alone and part of the Club Curve series. But there is mention of characters from my Mancini Legacy and Cimaruta MC Chicago series.

https://books2read.com/JustAsYouAre-ClubCurve

<u>Kostas</u>

Mating matches keep the peace in our world. So why did it feel like my life was over when it was my turn? She hated me from the moment we were paired. And to be honest? I hated her too. So when she rejected me for some loser from another clan, it didn't bother me that much. But then I met her—the one the fates chose for me—and everything just felt right. I knew in an instant that she was the one I would never let go of.

<u>Artemis</u>

In our world, mates can be either fated or chosen, but finding your fated mate is never guaranteed. I thought I had chosen someone who could love me and we would spend our lives together. But then he rejected me—for my BEST FRIEND. That day, I decided I was fine being alone. But then, completely by chance, I met someone who felt like home. Could this really be it? The forever I secretly craved...my fated one.

My Fated One is part of the Fated Mates Series. There is mention of characters from my Mancini Legacy Series and my Cimaruta MC Chicago Series.

https://books2read.com/MyFatedOne-FatedMates

Aiden

Motorcycle racing has been my life since I could walk and talk. It was all I ever needed. Or so I thought. Then I met the one woman that made me want more. One day, the unthinkable happens—a racing accident causes me to lose all my memories of her. But I still feel her in my soul, even if my brain can't remember her.

Élodie

I wanted a knight in shining armor, but what I got was a wolf in disguise. After escaping from him, I met a man willing to give me everything I ever wanted. Then in a split second, he was taken from me. Not physically, but mentally. The man I love doesn't remember who I am, but I'm determined to get him back.

Racing Back to Love is part of the Forget-Me-Not Series. There is mention of characters from my Mancini Legacy Series.

https://books2read.com/RacingBackToLove-ForgetMeNot

www.ingramcontent.com/pod-product-compliance
Lightning Source LLC
Chambersburg PA
CBHW022017310726
48972CB00006B/1688